JUST
LIKE
A REAL
PERSON

ALSO BY DOUG DIACZUK
Chalk

JUST LIKE A REAL PERSON

Doug Diaczuk

Winner of the 42nd Annual 3-Day Novel Writing Contest

ANVIL PRESS | VANCOUVER

Library and Archives Canada Cataloguing in Publication

Title: Just like a real person / Doug Diaczuk.
Names: Diaczuk, Doug, author.
Description: Winner of the 42nd annual 3-day novel-writing contest.
Identifiers: Canadiana 20210226919 | ISBN 9781772141764 (softcover)
Classification: LCC PS8607.I213 J87 2021 | DDC C813/.6—dc23

Book design by Derek von Essen
Represented in Canada by Publishers Group Canada
Distributed by Raincoast Books

The publisher gratefully acknowledges the financial assistance of the Canada Council for the Arts, the Canada Book Fund, and the Province of British Columbia through the B.C. Arts Council and the Book Publishing Tax Credit.

Anvil Press Publishers Inc.
P.O. Box 3008, Main Post Office
Vancouver, B.C. V6B 3X5 Canada
www.anvilpress.com

PRINTED AND BOUND IN CANADA

For A. J. P.

"It takes two to make an accident."
– F. Scott Fitzgerald, *The Great Gatsby*

I
MEET
LOLA

on an off-ramp, on the highway south of the city where three years ago two men and one woman died in a four-car pile-up caused by a drunk driver leaving a Christmas party where he drank gin and tonics all night and hit on co-workers by telling them how pretty they looked in green and red and smelling their necks and commenting on their perfume and how it reminded him of a girl he used to know in the city who smelled like lavender and roses or a teacher from ninth grade who inspired him to be an accountant and make money off of money, because the story had to be tailored to each woman he wanted to sleep with that night, and it's still up for debate as to whether or not he actually impressed or convinced or tricked any woman into sleeping with him, though most would argue that he struck out because when the paramedics arrived he was alone in his Mercedes Benz, his body twisted around the steering wheel and the smell of gin still coming off the last breaths he ever took, and the paramedics, or so I'm told, couldn't even be bothered to press their lips around his to breathe life into that alcohol-soaked body because they already knew a mother and father were dead and the kids in the back seat wouldn't stop crying, and this is what I tell Lola while we sit on the side of the road, leaning against the railing with nothing but darkness below us and flashing lights illuminating her yellow sundress and dark hair resting where the thin strap would be if it wasn't hanging halfway down her arm and covering a cut on the top of her shoulder where the glass from the windshield had flown through the air and sliced her skin when the impact happened just minutes ago, or hours, it's hard to tell when you've been in a car accident, at least that's what I've heard from other people because they all say that time kind of stands still, almost like a moment becomes an eternity or an eternity becomes a moment or some shit like that, and for the first time in my long and sorry life, I think I understand what they mean, because when Lola came into view in the headlights of my '94 Toyota Corolla on that off-ramp, her driving the wrong way, or me, I can't really remember, all I saw was her illuminated face through her windshield and I felt like, as sure as anything, that she was staring at me, my face lit up like a Christmas tree, pupils dilated as though I was looking at someone I loved, and then the impact, the headlights coming into contact first like a kiss, bursting and breaking, sparks flying, the electricity dispersing into the night and the light disappearing just as quickly as it appeared in that moment, and then nothing but darkness until the flashing lights of emergency vehicles lit up the night sky and flickered on the twisted metal of the cars and the broken glass lying on the road like Christmas lights hanging from houses that the women who work at accounting firms go home to after company parties and tell their husbands about how they were hit on by drunk co-workers who got behind the wheel stinking of gin and tonic and lime and perfume rubbed off their necks onto his, and their husbands scoff at the audacity of drunkards and how gin is an Englishman's drink that makes fools of even the most respectable men, but no man who drinks gin to excess could be considered respectable, that's what Lola says to me when I tell her about the drunk driver three years ago and I laugh and agree with her, because gin has never been my choice of drink, though I'm lying to her because I always love a gin and tonic on a hot summer night because there's just something so refreshing about it, but there is a time and a place to share your choice of drink with a woman you've just met, and I think better of it, so instead I tell her that there's a real decline in the class of drunk driver these days, because there used to be a time when half-full bottles of vodka or rum or whisky or even dozens of empty beer cans could be found inside vehicles that were flipped over on the sides of highways that made the gloves of firefighters sticky as they tried to pull out crippled and misshapen bodies of drunks from wrecks while cursing their stupidity and complete lack of discretion when it comes to the safety of others, but don't get me wrong, I'm no saint, I'm probably drunk now, and high on cocaine and alphazolam, diazepam, methanephines, and just for good measure, a fifth of vodka because I prefer that over gin, and besides, I didn't have any tonic and it isn't summer and I didn't need a refreshing drink to sip while sitting outside on a back porch looking at the scattered shards of stars in the suburban sky with a son and daughter, and a wife whose feet I massage while resting on my lap, because that's just a dream, or a delusion, or maybe even a nightmare depending on whose company you are in, and that's what Lola tells me, she tells me that dreams of suburban life are not dreams, they are nightmares because for most people, it is something that will inevitably come true and that's what nightmares really are, things that we think will never happen but we dream about them because it's our minds way of preparing us for things that could happen, so we have to be ready, just in case it comes true, and I'm not one to argue, so I agree with her and tell her that suburban life is for the weak and people who think they need something in their life to feel whole, but I don't need anything, just a fix, or a drink, or a smoke, or a blow job, or just a really good fucking car accident where people become mangled messes of human beings crumpled into unthinkable contortions that make the most seasoned firefighter or paramedic wince because humans aren't supposed to bend that way, and then I can slip in, after the bodies have been unravelled and made whole again, and gather up the twisted metal and the loose change now scattered amongst the floor mats and blood and search through gloveboxes for errant bills or drugs or unopened bottles of alcohol if I happen to come across a drunk driver, which is more often than not, and then take a moment to appreciate that so many goddamned fools crash their cars on highways while carrying things they would never want anyone to see or find, because we leave some of our most personal, our most embarrassing things in our cars because we don't expect anyone to ever find them, unless we turn them upside down, where everything spills out onto the road or is collected by tow truck drivers or even the odd brazen firefighter, and the best outcome you can hope for is that you die on impact and end up as one of those unrecognizable human puzzles that needs to be put back together by emergency crews, who in turn end up drinking and doing drugs just to handle all these deformed humans they encounter on a nightly basis, and who then end up as one of them, and I tell Lola that I love how everything is so cyclical, that those who end up cleaning up the messes of the lesser people who destroy their lives and their cars just end up becoming one of them because they can't handle the stress or the gravity of seeing a body in an unnatural state and Lola says it has nothing to do with the stress of seeing people like that because everyone is susceptible to giving into temptations and that there doesn't need to be any kind of precipitating trauma or gruesome scene, and I'm not sure if I believe her so I tell her that if I had to see things like this every day I would probably kill myself, and she doesn't know yet that I do see this kind of thing every day, but I want to see how she reacts, and she says that maybe that's for the best, and then she pushes herself off the railing of the off-ramp and walks away and I've never felt so rejected in my life, so I follow her and tell her that I thought she looked beautiful in the headlights of my car before we collided, but she doesn't turn around, so I keep following her, past the ambulance that treated us both for non-life-threatening injuries, and I tell Lola that I really like her dress, bloodstains and all, and she turns around, the little bit at the bottom lifting up to show the cut on the upper half of her thigh, and she asks me if I taste blood, and I do, and I touch my lip and try to see the red on my finger, against the red flashing lights, from a cut I now run my tongue over, and I savour the metallic taste and I tell her that it's sweet, like strawberries, and she knows I'm lying because there is blood on her lip too, and I wonder if we've kissed already or if it is from a piece of glass or from the airbag slamming into her face, which can kill you just as easily as your face slamming into the steering wheel, or so I've been told, and I wonder if there is any blood on the deflated bag in her car next to us from it hitting her face, and I think she is wondering this, too, because she looks over at her car, now combined with mine, and clearly we are not driving anywhere else tonight, so I ask her if she needs a ride, because the way she is casually moving further and further away from the scene I can tell she doesn't want to go to the hospital and neither do I, even though the paramedics said we should probably go just to be safe, but safety isn't on the top of my priority list and I want to get out of there as fast as I can and I just need Trevor to show up with the tow truck so I can slip into the cab and pretend like I was never part of this latest pile-up on the off-ramp like I have been so many times, and I think Lola feels the same way, because she walks up to me, so close I can see the blood on her lip, and she tells me that she needs to get as far away from here as she possibly can, so I tell her to follow me and we walk away from the scene until the flashing lights can't reach us anymore, and we hold hands on the side of the highway until I see the familiar lights of Trevor's tow truck and he pulls over, lets us in, and we sit in the cab and duck down when we return to the scene and wait for Trevor to peel Lola's car away from mine and load it onto the back of the truck and she keeps holding my hand and I can feel her breasts pressed into my chest and her hair on my face as she lies on top of me and we watch the flashing lights of ambulances and fire trucks on the cab roof go out one at a time and only the road flares burn in the night left by police looking for the drivers of the two cars who were just here a moment ago and who they spoke with briefly before returning to their cars to write it all down without realizing they just walked away, lost between all the bodies moving across the scene in

flashing lights that make everyone look the same, and just before
Trevor finishes, Lola turns her head to look at me and asks if I was
driving the wrong way or if she was and I tell her that I can't remember but that it doesn't matter, and I think she agrees, because she sits
up, tilts her head back, and licks the blood from her lips, just like I
do, and I can taste the blood and the iron inside it, and I lean my
head on her shoulder, near the cut from a piece of flying glass, and
tell her I love her, and Lola tells me that it's all my fault, and I tell
her she's right.

Everything is my fault.

I wake up with my head on the seat. It's still dark out. I sit up in
the cab of the tow truck and wipe the dried blood from my lips. I
feel the usual pangs of regret and denial that I've somehow done
something terribly wrong but don't care enough to figure out what
it was. There's a car on the back of the truck, its front crushed in
and the tires turned in ways tires shouldn't turn.

I need something to get me through the rest of the night, or
out of the truck, or to keep sitting upright. So I fall out onto the
pavement and taste blood again. I crawl onto the flatbed of the truck
to do what I usually do and search the glovebox and centre console
for money, jewellery, drugs, bottles of alcohol, whatever I can find.
But when I stand up, I see a woman in a yellow sundress sitting in
the driver's seat, hands on the steering wheel above the deflated
airbag, staring straight ahead out the shattered windshield.

I ask her what she's doing.

She doesn't answer. I try to open the passenger side door but it
won't budge so I crawl in through the window and sit in the passenger's seat that is pushed up nearly to the dash and my knees press
into my chin. Out of habit, I try to open the glovebox, but it's
stuck shut. The woman in the yellow sundress doesn't even turn
her head when I open the centre console and start to pull out the

maintenance manual and empty packs of gum and peppermints still in plastic wrappers and country music cassette tapes. On the bottom is a piece of scrap paper with an address written in pencil above a weekly schedule and a name.

I think her name is Lola.

Holding up the piece of paper I ask Lola if this means anything to her. She takes it and crushes it in her fist and doesn't even look at it before letting it drop to the floor mat. I ask her to pop the trunk but she doesn't answer. So I reach across her lap to find the release lever and she doesn't move. She stays perfectly still, looking straight ahead, hands on the steering wheel, and I can see her grip get tighter as though she's bracing for an impact. I notice she has blood on her dress from a cut on her leg intersecting an old scar that runs down to her knee. I can see her underwear. They're pink. I ask her if she was in an accident and if this is her car. She looks down at me and asks if I'm joking. I rest my head on her legs and find the trunk release latch and pull but I don't move because I like the view and the warmth coming from her bare legs below the edge of her dress.

You nearly killed me, she says.

I don't know what she's talking about but it sounds like something I'd do. I tell her I'm sorry and ask how she got that first scar that will now be overlapped by a new one. She tells me she was in a car accident but I think I already knew that and I tell her she should be more careful. She lifts her legs so my head hits the bottom of the steering wheel. It hurts more than it should have and I pull myself out from under the wheel and away from her legs and rub my ear and tell her that hurt.

Why are you doing this to me? she asks.

I'm not doing anything, I say. I don't even know what you're doing here.

She lifts up her dress to show me a cut on her upper thigh again and then she pulls down the left strap of her dress to show me a cut just above her collarbone, and then she pulls open her mouth with her fingers to show me her bloodstained teeth. Apparently I did these things to her, at least that's what she tells me.

I sit back up in the passenger seat and rest my head on the top of my knees and I tell her I'm sorry again. She doesn't even look at me so I start to pull myself out of the window and say I'm going to see if there's anything in the trunk.

My belt loop gets caught on some piece of the car that is in a place it shouldn't be and I'm hanging halfway out of the passenger side window. I ask Lola for a little help and she lets out a long sigh and then opens the driver-side door. The car chimes to alert the driver that the keys are still in the ignition. Lola comes around to my side and we are face to face, me hanging out of the car and her standing next to the truck, her arms folded across her chest. From here I can see down her dress and I'm happy her bra matches her underwear.

I'm Lola, she says and I tell her I know.

Do you remember anything from last night?

I tell her that I remember headlights, yellow sundresses, and broken glass.

Do you think you're funny?

Not particularly.

Were you drunk or stoned?

Probably.

How do you live with yourself?

One day at a time, I say.

I reach out my hands and ask her to pull, the car still chiming behind me because Lola didn't shut the door properly.

She grabs my hands and pulls me out of the car, the little piece of plastic that was holding on to me snapping, and I fall all the way to the pavement in the back of the impound lot. Lola is still holding my hands, or maybe I'm holding hers, but she doesn't pull away, so I use them to get up off the ground and we stand together like husband and wife about to kiss. She looks beautiful in the artificial light and I feel like I've seen her before, her face lit up, her pupils dilated like someone in love, but maybe they are now because the only light in the back lot is from a street light by the gate that pulses and flickers and attracts moths.

You're bleeding, Lola says, and not thinking, I let go of one of her hands to touch my bottom lip and look at the blood on my fingers. She uses this as an excuse to let go of my other hand and I'm filled with an incredible fear that I will never feel the touch of her skin again.

We walk to the back of the truck and I climb up onto the flatbed and hold out my hand to help her up, but she doesn't need my help and I feel sick.

There are two suitcases in the trunk of the car and one smaller bag. I ask Lola if they belong to her, but she doesn't answer. She just stares at them in the light from the little bulb somewhere inside the trunk that still works because the keys are still in the ignition.

Were you going on a trip somewhere? I ask.

No, I wasn't going anywhere, she says.

I ask her if she wants to check to make sure everything is okay and still here and she turns to me and says, you really don't remember, do you?

I wish I could tell her that it's all coming back to me, and if I'm being honest, there are always little snippets of past nights that flicker in my mind, like damaged film on a reel that flashes on a white screen, the most recent scenes from last night. Headlights, yellow sundress, broken glass, and the taste of blood on my lips.

I reach into the trunk and open up one of the suitcases. It is filled with pairs of pants, button-down shirts, and socks. I open the second suitcase and there are bags of cologne bottles that somehow didn't break and still smell quite lovely, paperback novels, and a photo album filled with images of water, children smiling, giant trees, and faded photographs of men in fine tailored suits and thick-rimmed glasses leaning against classic cars and smoking cigarettes.

There's one photo that shows a little girl gripping onto the shirt of a man. The photo is black and white and I can see the same shirt in the other suitcase. I ask Lola if she's the little girl but she doesn't even look at the photograph so I close the album and put it back.

I search through the two suitcases, looking in side pockets and reach my fingers all the way into the toes of the two pairs of shoes because that's where people often hide money. Lola doesn't touch anything and she just watches me search through someone else's life, or hers, but I think the men's underwear are too big for her.

I ask her what's in the smaller bag and she pulls it closer to us but doesn't open it. So I grab it and put it on top of the clothes in the larger suitcase and start to pull the zipper but Lola tells me to stop.

This isn't right, she says, and for the first time in a long time I feel guilty, but I don't tell her that I've made a semi-career out of searching through smashed-up cars, suitcases, duffle bags, jacket pockets, gloveboxes, and what remains of people's lives. Then she takes the bag from me and says we have to go to the hospital. I tell her I'm fine and ask if she's hurt. Lola touches the cut on her shoulder near her collarbone as though remembering the accident and says she forgot about it.

Do you have a car? she asks.

I don't drive.

The TV is still on but Trevor is asleep on the recliner in the break room. I tell Lola that I don't know if any of the cars in the lot still run and she tells me to just take all the keys hanging on the hooks on the wall.

The fourth car we try starts. It has a broken fender and it's missing the passenger side mirror, but otherwise it looks like it should be safe to drive. The radio doesn't work so we can't see the time, but the sky is turning that shade of purple that only people who work night shifts and the drug addicts on the street waking up on park benches and sidewalks starting to ache for the next fix get to see. I see this sky nearly every day and I tell Lola how beautiful I think it is, but she doesn't answer.

I try to make small talk. I tell her I like this time of day because there are so few cars on the road. I tell her that sometimes I like to drive down the middle of the street because it makes me feel like I'm the only person left on earth and not because I'm actually hoping for a head-on collision. I tell her that when I was six years old my dad wrapped a belt around my neck and hung me over the stairway banister until my face turned purple.

I'm sorry to hear that, she says.

It's not true, I say. Sorry, I didn't think you were listening.

We park in a No Parking zone and Lola cradles the bag in her arms and asks the nurse at the front counter about an old man who was brought here last night and I don't remember there being any old man in the car with her after the car accident on the off-ramp on the highway leading out of the city.

Seeing the blood, the nurse asks if we are okay, and we tell her that we are fine. I don't think she believes us. She tells us to take a seat and I ask Lola if she has any change for the vending machine. I need to get something in my body, even if it's just sugar. Lola just stares at me and says, let me just reach into my pocket, and then rolls her eyes.

Check the bag, I say. Maybe there's some money inside.

No.

Then I will.

Lola slaps my hand away and tells me to sit down.

What am I thinking. I'm in a hospital. There's so much more than sugar. So I tell Lola I have to go to the bathroom and I'll be right back. She doesn't say anything and I think she would prefer if I just left.

Rats have an unjustified bad reputation. If I was to be bitten by a radioactive animal, I wouldn't choose a spider or a bat or a lion. I would want to be bitten by a radioactive rat because rats can slip into so many places unseen. So can I, but I'm no rat. In Grade 9 I stopped the door to the teachers' lounge from closing with my foot after the principal walked out and I slipped inside without anyone seeing. I spent the rest of fourth period drinking cup after cup of coffee and making origami swans from torn out pages of magazines. Then I threw up and left without anyone knowing it was me.

Unfortunately, hospitals are not as quiet as the streets at this time of day or teachers' lounges during fourth period, so it's harder to catch closing doors with my foot, and when I do, the rooms are not empty.

But like the little rat that I am, I manage to find an empty room, unlocked, and inside I have my pick of morphine; antidepressants, fluoxetine, benzodiazepine, venlafaxine, and desvenlafaxine; anticoagulants; sleeping pills; adrenaline; oxycodone; and rubbing alcohol.

I decide on a mixture of benzodiazepine and painkillers and pocket a couple vials of morphine for later.

Back in the waiting area, Lola is gone and I ask the nurse behind the desk if the woman in the yellow sundress left. The nurse says she's in the back getting treatment and she asks me again if I'm okay and if I need to see a doctor. I tell her it's just some cuts and bruises and slip in through the doors to the back when she's not looking.

I didn't think it was that bad, Lola says when I find her sitting on the edge of a bed. She lowers the strap of her dress and shows me the stitches near her collarbone. I tell her I'm sorry but I'm not entirely sure why.

I ask her if the old man is here.

I'm not sure, Lola says. I think he's already gone.

It happens, I say, and then ask if he was in the car with her.

Lola looks away. I think she might be crying. She picks up the bag and holds it in her lap, pulling at the zipper with her fingers but not hard enough to make it move.

It's all my fault, she says, and now I can see that she is crying. Everything is my fault.

I MET LOLA ON AN OFF-RAMP,
on the highway leading south out of the city, this is what she tells me as she runs her fingers over the bandage covering the stitches holding the cut closed near her collarbone and she tells me it doesn't hurt, but I can see in her face that it does, and I wonder what it's like to feel pain because right now I don't feel anything thanks to the painkillers lifted from a hospital cabinet and if this car was to crash and I was ejected out through the windshield because I'm not wearing a seatbelt in order to turn my body so it's facing Lola, I don't think I would feel the glass cutting through my face or my skin being left on the pavement or my bones being crushed by the impact, and I tell Lola that I'm completely numb and I like being numb because it makes me just feel like a body without a mind or a mind without a body and it makes getting up in the morning, or the evening, or the afternoon a little easier, and I think she thinks I'm crazy, but then she tells me I'm one of the lucky ones and that she remembered my face in the headlights from her car and she swears I was smiling, even though I don't remember smiling, but I like to think Lola was when her face came into view through the headlights of my '94 Toyota Corolla, less than six hours ago, when we first met and the light went dark in an instant, and I tell her I love her again because I don't know what else to say and it feels like the right thing to say, but she doesn't say anything for a really long time, so I tell her that I really like this time of day when the sun is barely up because all these people sitting in their cars during the morning commute are all the same and that it's really

no different than running down the middle of an empty street at four in the morning because all these people in their cars might as well not even be there, because they hardly have a presence of mind to know just how similar they are to the person in the car next to them, and they are all just driving mindlessly to a mindless job hoping they don't get into an accident caused by some careless driver or drunk going to work after staying up until five in the morning drinking, and I tell Lola that this is the best time for car accidents because it's when people are the most unhappy and even the prospect of smashing a car head-on with one coming down the road in the opposite direction is more appealing than getting to wherever it is they are going, and as I'm saying all this, unable to keep my mouth shut, Lola says I love you, too, and then she finds a gap in the traffic in the opposite lanes and starts driving up an off-ramp in the wrong direction and she is smiling the whole time, right up until the unmistakable sound of metal colliding with metal, and glass sprinkling across the pavement, and the sweet smell of gasoline and the bitter taste of blood, and Lola, who doesn't stop laughing.

I
MET
TREVOR

in a convenience store parking lot, on the city's north side in a neighbourhood full of the human garbage that gets tossed out by the people who have no use for drug addicts and single mothers and ex-convicts and dealers and children with donation bin clothes and sneakers two sizes too big, the kind of place where people like me can feel like kings among lesser beings because I'm probably the worst of them all because I love every single goddamned minute of it, and it's not just because I was there in only body and not in mind, my mind being that of a high school dropout hooked on cocaine, crack, heroin or whatever drug I could get my hands on by the time I was eighteen years old, convincing me to rob convenience stores by twenty-one, and slipping away under the street lights one by one, and making deals in back alleyways and falling in love in parking lots, and just being an all around amazing person, and that's when Trevor found me, in a parking lot where two cars kissed head-on following an argument between two men over the last malt liquor on the shelf and the one not letting the other leave, so rather than act like actual human beings, they decided to just crash their cars into each other and Trevor came to clean up the mess and haul one of the cars away on his flatbed tow truck, one of the many unseen heroes in this world who make things we don't want to see disappear, things like wrecked cars, discarded needles, dead bodies, shit stains on the walls of public bathrooms in fast-food restaurants, and anything else that reminds people there are others worse off than they are, and I admire people like Trevor because someone has to do it, so they might as well make the best of it, and Trevor has made the best of everything, he always has, and when he pulled into the parking lot, glanced at the cars, and took his pick, he called over to me standing by the front doors of the store, sipping a Big Gulp bought for me by a group of greasy teenagers who wanted me to buy them smokes and liquor, which I did for a little extra cash, and they were more grateful than they should have been because they don't see how stupid they really look or sound when they ask someone like me to do something like that, but I don't care, I don't mind helping out the downtrodden who are just looking for a little something to feel anything, though when I was a teenager, I preferred to just lift things off the shelves and run out of the place, rather than suffer the indignity of having to ask a crackhead or a heroin addict or a drunk to go into a convenience store in the middle of the afternoon to buy

me shit at double the price and cross my fingers that the addict or
drunk wouldn't just run off with the cash like I have so many times,
but they will learn one day and I hope they look back on this day
and remember my disapproving looks and the shame they must
have felt, perhaps mixed with a little bit of excitement too of knowing they were going to go get drunk down the bike trails that lead
to the river and get sick from smoking too many regular cigarettes,
and sometimes I wish they would invite me to come along just so I
could watch it all unfold, but I figure I do enough just helping them
get to that point, even if I look down on them like the parasites that
they are, but I still felt rather proud of myself, and a little important,
as I leaned against the wall of that convenience store and watched
the entire ballet unfold in the parking lot between two drunks
looking for that last bottle of malt liquor, and if it wasn't for me,
none of this would have happened, because I bought the second-last
one for those teenagers right before the two cars pulled up to the
store, so I almost felt like what I was watching was my very own
play, one I wrote and directed and offered stage directions for when
I told one of the drivers not to put up with that shit from the other,
and then in act 2 the police were called and both men were arrested
and taken away, and the bottle of malt liquor was just sitting there
in one of the cars, and in the final act, when Trevor called to me
and asked me to help him secure a chain to the frame of the car
under the crushed-in fender, I became the star, a god descending
from above the curtain on destroyed machines, and after the car
was loaded onto the flatbed of the truck, Trevor opened the passenger door and grabbed the bottle, because he always chooses the
right car, and he asked me if I wanted a drink, and I'm not going to
say no to that because to be honest, I'm no better than those greasy
teenagers with pockmarked faces and cash stolen from their mother's
purses, I'm just smart enough to know I'm already a piece of shit
and they still have that lesson to learn, so Trevor and I pass the
bottle of malt liquor back and forth and he tells me he loves towing

cars from convenience store parking lots or liquor stores or back alleys on the north side of town because there's always something inside that he can either use or sell and I remember being both impressed by his initiative and a little grateful that I could never get my life together enough to actually own a car, but apparently the best place to find what he calls a jackpot or a treasure chest or a golden nugget is on highways leading in and out of the city because that's where you find people who have packed up everything and are trying to leave everything else behind, or coming here to make a fresh start, it's the transition, he said, that makes these accidents the most lucrative, but you have to choose the car you're going to pick up carefully, because you could just as easily end up with some random car driving down the highway on the way back to the city from a country club just beyond the city limits or suburban families returning home from a night out at a chain restaurant, in which case you only find food from doggy bags staining the seats and the roof of the minivan and piss and shit stains from kids who got scared from the impact, but it's the cars leaving the city or coming in that have life savings tucked into the toes of shoes packed in suitcases, all the prescription medications needed to keep a person alive, and family heirlooms hidden in the pockets of packed clothes to keep them safe, and it's not like anyone is even going to notice something is missing because they have far more important things on their minds, things like shattered femurs, punctured lungs, lacerated spleens, and the likelihood that they may never walk again, or they're dead, in which case rarely does anyone come looking for what might or might not have been inside an upside down car, or one that is barely even recognizable as a car, but these little treasure chests are not always the easiest to find, because despite what you might think from reading the newspapers or watching the evening news, traffic accidents don't happen all that often, unless you can make them happen, and that's where I fit into Trevor's little business venture, a numb, senseless, useless piece of human garbage who can get behind the wheel and be willing to swerve into the oncoming lane and then help pick through what's left of the lives I shatter, and over the years I've been lucky, like those faceless dummies put in cars that are driven into walls to make sure the airbags will save a life or the seatbelts don't snap on impact and then they are put back together to do it over and over again, or maybe it's because my body is already so numb that it goes limp, and I'm like one of those drunk or stoned drivers you read about in the newspapers who walk away from terrible accidents unhurt that people really wish had died on impact because it's what they deserve or someone high school students are warned about becoming during assemblies because you might not die but you could kill someone else, and so far I'm not aware of having killed anyone because I've learned when to turn, how to brake just before impact, and when to hit the gas at just the right moment, though I've never followed up on any other drivers or read the papers or stopped by any hospitals during visiting hours, but I hope all those who have come into contact with me can see past the years of physiotherapy or post-traumatic stress or painkiller addiction that arises from the accident to see the gift I've given them and what it means to be alive, because our bodies can be repaired and our minds can forget, but we can't save ourselves from the worst injury we inflict upon ourselves every day, denial, and as for me, so far my worst injuries have been two broken wrists, a collapsed lung, six concussions, three broken noses, a tongue nearly bit in half, three broken toes, a pinky finger that won't bend past ninety degrees, internal bleeding, ongoing and persistent denial, and once my heart stopped, but I was brought back to life by a plucky paramedic who recognized me from treating a burst blood vessel in my left eye after an impact with a station wagon that I couldn't resist because it had one of those luggage carriers on top of the roof, and then again after I rear-ended a sedan that looked like it had a full back seat of bags and boxes, but it turned out it was just donations being made to a homeless shelter in the next city, and I had to be treated for whiplash, and this paramedic asked me why I keep getting into so many car accidents and I told her that I guess I'm just an unlucky person, and she suggested that maybe I should give up driving, and I told her she's probably right, but she didn't know that I didn't even have a driver's license, and neither do the police, who, if I'm not able to sneak away soon enough, will ask to see my license and I tell them I keep it in the glovebox and when they check and say it isn't there, I just tell them it must have been thrown from the car during the impact, or if it's a minor wreck, and my body allows, I worm my way into the passenger seat and tell them I can't remember who was driving, but if the impact is bad enough, if the car is in rough enough shape, they usually believe whatever I say if I'm behind the wheel because I'm a really trustworthy person and car accidents are so traumatic and usually assigned to the rookie cops for traffic control, that no one really wants to give you the third degree especially if you are gasping for air as though it's your last breath or screaming that you can't feel your legs, so not only am I a really trustworthy person, I'm also a really good fucking liar, and I love reenacting the pained screams I've heard from so many others, and I usually manage to avoid questions about how much I've had to drink tonight or if I've done any drugs lately and by the time everything settles down, and I'm not in an ambulance, I'm usually just gone, alive to go and get in a wreck another day, and that way Trevor and I can keep living off the scraps of the discarded lives, of the things people put in cars thinking those things are safer than they will ever be and they also don't realize a heavy box in the back seat of a car can kill you when it flies forward after you collide head-on with another car that brakes early as though anticipating the impact, but I don't remember any braking the last time, when a woman in a yellow sundress was behind the wheel, and I'm totally fucked up on the painkillers being fed into my veins from an IV next to the hospital bed that Trevor examines with his stubby fingers, asking me if it's any good and if I want any of the stronger stuff, but I tell him it's doing the trick and I ask him if he went to pick up the car, it was his after all, and he said he was there, and he got the car and brought it back to the lot, but when I ask him about the woman in the yellow sundress, he said he didn't see anyone, but a paramedic on the scene told him that two people were transported to hospital with life-threatening injuries, not including me, because my life wasn't threatened, but my heart sinks a little, at least I think it does, the painkillers make it hard to tell if its even beating, but I do feel it sinking down into the soles of my feet, and I tell Trevor that I remember someone laughing and ask him if the paramedic said anything about laughter, and he replies that it sounds like the nurses did give me the strong stuff and then turns the little dial on the hose, and before I drift off into sleep with the sound of shattering glass and laughter still echoing my head, I ask Trevor if he found a bag in the car, but he tells me it was empty.

Just like me.

When I wake up Trevor is gone and so is my IV bag but the needle is still in my hand. Without the painkillers pumping into my blood I can feel what I'm guessing are broken ribs, maybe even a punctured lung, and it feels like my knee is bending in the wrong direction.

Someone is standing in the doorway wearing a dark uniform and she sees that I'm awake and comes inside. It's the same paramedic who suggested I give up driving and she says, fourth time's the charm and I try to smile, but I don't tell her that this is actually my forty-second time, but the first one where I wasn't behind the wheel.

Shouldn't that be connected to something, she asks, pointing to the needle sticking out of the top of my hand and a hose going nowhere. I tell her that I think someone stole it and she says she will go get the nurse but I tell her not to worry about it and that the pain is good for me because I've forgotten what it feels like.

She holds up her hand and there is a small piece of paper in between her finger and thumb.

I found this in the car, she says. I thought it might be important.

She walks into the room and places it on the small table beside me and says she's never had to pull the same person out of a smashed vehicle more than once, let alone four times.

I tell her I appreciate her efforts and her dedication to the job and apologize for making her work so much. She laughs and I tell her she has a pretty smile and then she turns her head away. The name above her right breast says E. Shaw.

Do you know what's wrong with me? I ask.

I know you had two broken ribs and your right knee was hyperextended, but I don't think anything broke or tore, but I'm sure the doctors will do more X-rays and tests. You also had a lot of glass in your face and I thought maybe you were blinded in your right eye, but I think it was just because there was a lot of blood.

Then she tells me I'm lucky to be alive because the car was a real mess, all twisted and bent.

How do you do it? I ask Shaw.

It's my job.

That's not what I asked. I asked how you do it.

Shaw sits down on the edge of the bed and tells me that she just treats every single call like the one before it.

I don't see people, she says. I see situations, I see injuries, I see bleeding that needs to be stopped, I see bones that need to be set, and hearts that need to be restarted. You're the first real person I can remember seeing.

This is the first time I've ever been called a real person. Shaw takes it one step further by touching my arm with her hand and telling me that she hopes I'll make a full recovery.

I just wanted to see how you were doing, she says, and then takes her hand away but I wish she kept it there because I could feel the warmth of her skin on mine and for the first time in my life I was thankful nothing was coursing through my veins and numbing my body.

Before she leaves, I ask her about a woman in a yellow sundress and if she made it. Shaw says there was no woman in a yellow sundress and that I was the only one in the car.

But I wasn't driving.

You were behind the wheel, Shaw says. I pulled you out myself. Get some rest. I'll send the nurse.

Was there a bag in the car? I ask.

I have no idea, Shaw says. I don't concern myself with what's in the car. Only the people.

And little scraps of paper? I ask.

I'm pretty sure it's important.

Then she picks up the piece of paper she just put down, turns it over, and writes something on the back and places it on my chest and tells me to call her if I need to talk.

Before she leaves, I ask Shaw if she can do me one little favour. She stops at the door and says, anything. So I ask her to say she found me in the passenger side of the car. I can tell this makes her uncomfortable, but she agrees.

The nurse comes a little bit after Shaw leaves and seems puzzled by the missing IV bag and I tell her I have no idea what happened because I was asleep the entire time. She asks me on a scale of one to ten how bad the pain is and I tell her it's eleven. She adds a new bag and makes sure the needle is still in place and I can feel the warmth enter my veins, not unlike a hand resting on my forearm.

A police officer comes later and says a paramedic told him I was found in the passenger seat and asks me who was driving the car. I say it was a woman. When he asks for a description, I tell him she was wearing a dress, but I can't remember the colour.

I didn't know her, I reply to his next question. I had just met her that night.

After everyone is gone, I look at the paper Shaw found in the car. On one side is a phone number. On the other there is an address, a weekly schedule, and a name. I think she told me her name was Lola.

I MEET TREVOR IN THE HOSPITAL PARKING LOT, on the west side of the city, after checking myself out early against medical advice like I have so many times before, crutches tucked under my arms to keep weight off my knee that was hyperextended so much I tore two ligaments, and I'm still wearing the hospital gown because Shaw had to cut off my shirt to examine my broken ribs and make sure one hadn't punctured my lungs, and I'm assuming every move I make is registered as pain somewhere in my body, but the painkillers prescribed to me that I carry in an oversized orange bottle keep those messages from reaching my brain, and that's just fine by me, because I really like keeping things my body feels away from my brain, otherwise I wouldn't be able to do half the things I do, and my brain seems okay with letting things slide and my body bearing the brunt of the choices I've made in life, the worst one probably being getting in Trevor's tow truck in that convenience store parking lot so many years ago, but I didn't know any better and I still don't, because despite what Shaw says, I'm not a real person, I'm more of an idea, a concept, or maybe I'm just the fucked up part of some fuck-up's dream, because when you get right down to it, I feel nothing, not even pain, and the only emotion I ever feel is love because it's better than any drug, and I don't even have a past, not that I can remember anyway, I just wake up like every day is the first day of my life, and I love it, and I wish more people could know what that feels like, because I have nothing to weigh me down, no memories of childhood traumas, no heartbreak to keep me from falling in love one day at a time, or anxieties about any pre-existing health conditions that might otherwise make me second-guess myself when it comes to taking certain medications or never touching alcohol because of a predisposition toward alcoholism, none of that matters to me, none of that exists for me, so I just keep going, one day at a time, agreeing to purposefully crash cars for Trevor in the hopes of finding someone's life savings, or drugs, or guns, or whatever else he can pawn off for a little extra money on top of what he makes in the towing business, it's not my concern and I don't really care how other people make their money, just as long as I can get a little to keep me going, to keep putting one day in front of the other until that final crash when there are no more days left and I'll never feel pain or numbness again and the world will keep turning with all the real people still on it, carrying around their pasts like stones that rest on the shoulders of Greek gods, and constantly worrying that the driver in the next lane over will fall asleep at the wheel and cross the centre line and cause a massive pileup and kill them and their three children while on a family road trip, or a drunk driver will blow through a stop sign and kill an elderly couple who have never been in a car accident after sixty years of driving, and it can't be me, I can't be the one responsible for all these accidents, other people do a fine job without me, like sixteen-year-olds in family station wagons running red lights, inattentive drivers sideswiping minivans that end up upside down in ditches, degenerates purposefully looking to hurt themselves to escape the pain they already feel, which is why I really am so inconsequential, but I think that's what Trevor saw in me, just how little I thought of myself and other people, and because he thinks so little of me, why not use me to get him a little extra business and find the best cars to get the best things, and really it's more of a game for the both of us, him seeing how long I can keep this up, smashing all the cars in his impound lot that were never claimed and that he fixed up just to smash them again, and me, seeing how long it will take until the big crash comes, sending me through the windshield at sixty kilometres per hour headed directly for a woman's face, now dark after the headlights explode, her pupils dilated, and me flying toward her lips first, wanting nothing more than to break through the glass and taste the blood on her lips, and as I enter the driver's side and smell her perfume, I look down at her dress.

It's always a yellow sundress.

I
MEET
SHAW

at a coffee shop on the city's south side, the one that was held up at gunpoint last year by a junkie wearing a Halloween mask of Michael Myers and the only thing I remember thinking is why didn't he use a knife, and how much did he honestly expect to get from a coffee shop on the city's south side, but caffeine is a drug and people pay big money for drugs, and I should know because I dropped thirty dollars on three hits of acid yesterday, forgetting that I still had my third refill of prescription painkillers in my jacket pocket along with Shaw's number that she wrote down on a piece of paper found in the remains of the latest broken car that I wasn't even driving and left on the table beside my hospital bed, so I decide to only take four painkillers and half a hit of acid before calling Shaw and asking if she wants to meet because I need someone to talk to, and she tells me she knows a place and I catch the next bus and stare out the window wishing I was behind the wheel of every single one of the cars passing by, my foot pumping imaginary gas pedals but never hitting the brake, and I arrive thirty minutes late and find her sitting in a booth stirring her coffee with one of those long plastic straws while staring out the window, and at first I don't recognize her without her uniform on, but she sees me first and waves me over and asks what I would like, but I say I don't drink coffee because I can't handle the caffeine, and this makes her smile and I decide that my new favourite thing is making her smile because she has very pretty teeth and full lips and I try to remember what they felt like against mine and I kind of wish my heart had stopped the night of my most recent car accident so she would have had to breathe life back into my body again, her lips to mine, but unfortunately my heart kept beating, though I still have the rest of the painkillers in my pocket, so if I take them all, along with the two-and-a-half hits of acid to make the experience more exhilarating, she will have to bring me back to life and she won't have a choice because that's her job, and that's what I tell her after sitting down, not that I want her to breathe life back into my overdosing body, but that I admire and respect her job, and I even tell her that I've seen paramedics at work many times, but stop myself before revealing that it's because I've been in dozens of car accidents in the last eight years, and luckily she doesn't ask any follow-up questions, aside from what it is I needed to talk about, and the truth is, I didn't need to talk to anyone because I never need to talk to anyone, but I wanted to talk to her, so I lie and tell her that I've been having a really hard time since the accident, and I tap the crutches leaning against the booth to emphasize my point that I'm still struggling with the injuries, even though I don't even feel them and if it wasn't for the fact that my knee would give out, my body not listening to what my brain is telling it, I wouldn't even be using the crutches, but I'd rather not have to pull myself across the sidewalk like some invalid while the real people in this city step on or over me, ignoring this non-person, but Shaw doesn't see me this way, she sees a real person, a broken person she's had to pull from broken cars on four separate occasions, and I can't help but think that that puts us in some kind of strange, co-dependent relationship where she's the hero and I'm the victim and I've never played the hero before because I do such a good job as the victim, and Shaw keeps on being the hero when she asks me if there is anything she can do to help me with my injuries or move on from my most recent automotive mishap, and the truth is, she actually can, because there is more from that night that has stuck with me than the torn ligaments in my knee and the bruises on my chest and the cuts on my face, there is an even greater injury in my brain that I can't completely numb, no matter how many painkillers I take, and I can't drown it in alcohol because I always just end up waking with the thought of yellow sundresses and broken glass and collarbones covered in blood, so I ask Shaw if she's sure that she doesn't remember a woman being there, and she says she doesn't but tells me this isn't the first time I've asked her that and every time she's pulled me from a car I've asked her about another woman being there, but she says it's funny because people always seem to think someone else is there, whether there is or not, and she tells me about one of the first accidents she ever attended where there was a woman in the passenger seat of a car, she was thirty-five years old and unresponsive, and I ask Shaw if she tried to help the woman, and she doesn't answer right away and just stirs her coffee, then she says you always focus on the patient that stands the best chance of surviving, so I checked on the driver of the other car and he was conscious and while I was trying to calm him down, telling him that everything will be okay, he kept asking about a woman but not the one in the passenger seat, and Shaw says she didn't know if he meant the driver of the other car or if he thought there was a woman sitting next to him, for all I know she was ejected from the car, Shaw says, or sitting against a guard rail waiting for treatment, people end up in the strangest places following accidents, so I ask why she didn't go looking for the other woman, picturing it as some sick game of hide and seek, but she had already made her choice based on survivability, so I ask about the other woman in the passenger side of the car, suggesting that maybe if she got there quicker, if she chose differently, she would have survived, and I can tell my phrasing upsets her and I admit it is a poor choice of words and really does sound like I'm blaming her for a woman's death, but she tells me it's okay when I apologize and that she never went over there because someone else was already attending to the woman, who was unconscious and not breathing, and she and her partner had to perform CPR all the way to the hospital in the back of the ambulance, trading off every ten minutes, and he was really upset when he learned she died the next day, and I ask Shaw if losing a patient upsets her, and she just shrugs her shoulders and says it comes with the job, you can't save everyone, she says, no matter how hard you try, and I start to wonder what she's on, what's making her so numb inside, but I don't ask that, instead I ask if the second woman was ever found, but she says she can't remember and once she leaves a scene, the only way to return to it is in her memory, which happens more often than she'd care to admit, so I ask her if she ever wants to quit her job, but she says she couldn't imagine doing anything else, so I tell her I respect that and I admire her, and then I tell her she's very beautiful and she smiles again and it's still my favourite thing to do, and I ask her if she wants to get out of here and get really high and have sex for the rest of the day.

I've been clean for five years, she says.

She touches me like I'm made of glass. Either she's afraid I'll break or she doesn't want to cut herself when I do.

I don't want to hurt you, she says.

It's fine, I tell her. I can't feel anything.

What kind of painkillers do they have you on?

I tell her the bottle is in my jacket pocket and she walks across the bedroom naked and reads the label before asking me how many I've taken.

Today?

Yes.

What does it say?

Two in the morning.

I took two in the morning.

I don't tell her that I took four in the morning, then another on the bus ride to the coffee shop.

These are pretty strong, she says and I tell her they are really helping with the pain. She puts the bottle away and crawls back into bed.

I ask her how she got clean and she tells me that she had no choice, it was either stop taking pills or lose her job and probably end up dead, so one day she just stopped, just like that, no more pills for E. Shaw.

I can't tell if I admire that or if she is lying. I want to believe it's that easy to just give something up and move on to a happy life, but when I ask her if she's happy, she doesn't answer. I love when people can't answer such a simple question. It's like trying to decide if you're happy is like trying to decide if you're crazy. No one can really tell on the outside, and you can't really tell on the inside either because it could just be a lie we tell ourselves or a lie we've created through copious amounts of drugs and alcohol.

Shaw asks if I'm okay and I tell her I am. So she breathes more life into my body by touching her lips to mine and she gently climbs on top of me and I tell her to be careful, I might crack, and she is and I do.

I lick the beads of sweat from between her breasts and I ask if she has a yellow sundress. She doesn't because she doesn't like the way bright colours make her look.

What did you see that morning? she asks me.

A woman in a yellow dress, I say. She kept laughing and she had a bag in her lap.

Sometimes our brains make up stories and images when we experience something traumatic, Shaw says. It's almost like an escape. Maybe you have a pleasant memory of someone in a yellow dress that your brain just thought of because you were afraid.

The only memory I have of yellow dresses involve car crashes, I say.

Then maybe that's why you thought you saw it.

The sweat from her breasts tastes bitter and I kiss her lips trying to remember the taste of blood, but instead they taste sweet.

What if she was really there? I ask.

What if she was?

I guess it doesn't matter, I say. Then I excuse myself to go to the bathroom and she helps me the whole way and I feel like an old man, and if I do make it to old age, I hope all the nurses are naked when they help you to the bathroom.

I ask Shaw to bring me my jacket and shirt and I decide to take a full hit of acid and two more painkillers. When I come out, Shaw is getting dressed, thinking my asking for my clothes was a not-so-subtle sign that I wanted to leave. I don't want to leave and I ask her if I can stay. She stops buttoning up her shirt. I think she likes the company as much as I like making her smile. So we get back into bed and I kiss her on the lips and with the tip of my tongue I pass the acid onto hers and she doesn't stop me.

I MET SHAW AT A COFFEE SHOP ON THE CITY'S SOUTH SIDE, and then we went back to her apartment and made cautious love for hours while I cracked and nearly shattered to pieces between the sheets, and then we got really fucked up and became convinced that the bed was floating on water that kept rising in the apartment and we would float up to the ceiling and be crushed to death, and even though the ceiling always looks like it's getting closer and closer, we never reach it, and Shaw can't stop laughing and I tell her to be quiet, but she doesn't listen, and sometimes when I look up at her jumping up and down on the bed naked she is wearing a yellow sundress and blood drips down from a cut on her leg and runs down her arm from a gash on her shoulder near her collarbone, so I have to close my eyes, I have to keep my eyes closed and pretend I don't see her and that the motion on the bed, which is causing me to crack even more, is just the movement of a car gliding silently down the highway, not looking for anything in particular, not any cars coming to the city or leaving, with life savings tucked into shoes and family heirlooms hidden under bras, but just driving for the sake of driving, to get away, to leave everything behind, and when I do that, I won't be carrying anything, no luggage, no bags, not even a goddamn wallet because I don't have a license to drive a car anyway, and the only cash I earn is what I find in the wrecks of cars, so I will just keep on driving, hoping there isn't some other moral degenerate out there like me that cares so little about real people that he is willing to deliberately crash a car into them just to try and score some loose change or drugs or alcohol in bottles that don't break, and really, just to see if he's still alive because there's no way to tell really unless you are constantly on the brink of death, and it makes me wonder what it will be like when it actually finds me, what I will think, if I will even believe it, because I've come so close so many times, why should I believe it when it actually does, and I ask Shaw what it's like to see someone die, and the car stops on the highway, either because it collided with someone else, or because I slam on the brakes, either way, there's nothing but flashing lights going in all directions, and Shaw tells me it's terrifying to watch someone die, especially when you're trying to save them, because it's almost like you've failed, she says, like every single moment in their life was leading up to that moment with you, where you are supposed to save them, you are supposed to restart their heart, stop the bleeding, keep the drugs from preventing the brain from send-ing signals telling the fucking loser to keep breathing, and then it all stops with you, and you just have no idea what to do with that, so you do nothing but steal prescription medications from work and start taking them like candy and numb yourself from anything and everything until you no longer see people, you just see injuries, symptoms, scars, and medications, and it makes life a lot easier when you have a job helping people but don't see them as people anymore, and she tells me this while standing over me naked and I've never felt so small and vulnerable before, if I wasn't already made of glass, I would have been made of sand, and fallen apart on the bed sheet as she rocked back and forth on her heels on the mattress, bringing the car back to life, and I tell her, let's go, let's drive this motherfucking thing to the end of the goddamn earth and not hit a single car just to prove that we can, and she asks me what I'm talking about, so against my better judgement, I tell her that I intentionally get into car accidents to steal things left behind and tell myself that in order to be alive we have to be closer to death, and then she jumps down, her knees landing on each side of me, and the car is really picking up speed now, I can feel it, I can feel being pushed back into the seat from the force and the windows must be open because I can barely breathe, and I can feel Shaw pressing into my body and I can't help but get an erection and ask her if she wants to fuck and I promise her that I won't shatter into a million little pieces, but all she says is she'll show me what it feels like to die, and I'm finding it harder and harder to breathe, but I try to laugh and I ask her again if she has a yellow sundress, and then she lets go of my throat and she starts to laugh, too, and she says she thinks she just might, and she jumps off me, and it turns out I was inside her after all, and when she comes back, she's wearing a long, yellow rain jacket that goes past her knees, and she tells me to follow her because she thinks she hears the rain, but I tell her it's just the water rising from the floor and trying to push us to the ceiling, but she is already out the door, and I fumble with my crutches and follow her, and I have to wait for the elevator, and when I reach the lobby I realize I'm only wearing my jacket and naked from the waist down, but I can see the yellow coat outside the front doors spinning around in the lights from the street and the passing cars, and when I get outside I see the headlights of an oncoming car break when they collide with Shaw, and she flies over the top of the car and lands in the middle of the road, and this is the moment I decide to get clean, so I take the prescription painkillers from my pocket, pop off the lid, and swallow whatever's left.

There's no sense letting them go to waste.

I MEET MYSELF IN A HOSPITAL ON THE CITY'S EAST SIDE, the same hospital I found myself in several weeks ago recovering from injuries sustained in a car accident that I didn't even cause and made a woman in a yellow sundress disappear, and I can't be certain what's inside the IV bag dripping into my veins through the needle stuck in my hand, and though it makes my skin tingle I'm still fully aware of the pain radiating throughout my body and my brain and I have to admit, if this is what living feels like, I'd rather be dead, and apparently I was, that's what the doctor tells me when he comes in and reads from my chart, telling me how they had to pump my stomach from an overdose of prescription pain medication that made my heart stop not once, but three times, and I'm very lucky to be alive, because if it wasn't for the paramedics who were responding to a pedestrian collision on the street in front of the sidewalk where I collapsed, I would have been dead, and I tell the doctor that that wouldn't have been such a bad thing, and this was the wrong thing to say, because he tells me he will refer me to a psychiatrist, and that explains why my hands and legs are strapped to the bed, but I tell the doctor I'm not crazy, I'm just in the process of getting clean and I'm not one to let anything go to waste, and he closes my chart and says next time I should just dump the pills down the toilet and not my throat, and I thank him for the advice, because it really is the best advice I have ever received, and I mean it, not a lot of people give me advice, let alone good advice, and I want to return the favour, so I tell the doctor that when it comes to telling me about an accident on the street in front of the sidewalk, maybe ask me first if I knew the person, so he asks me if I did, and I say I didn't, and I ask if she is okay, but he doesn't know, and that's that, he leaves the room and I'm still strapped to the bed, being fed some kind of concoction through an IV that I can only assume is a mixture of antidepressants and anti-anxiety medication that really isn't a dose I'm used to, but maybe getting clean is a matter of weaning myself off a little bit at a time, because this is the new me, the clean me, the sober me, no more snorting, injecting, inhaling, drinking anything else, from here on out, right after the IV is pulled from my hand, I'm going to be clean and sober, and I will only crash cars if it is outside of my control, and it's that loss of control that hits me like a semi-truck head-on in the fast lane, because I've never had to be in control of my own life, things have always just happened, whether I wanted them to or not, and I didn't care if they did, the only control I ever really had was deciding when to turn into the oncoming lane, and now that's not up to me, I have to just keep driving straight, keeping the lines on either side of the car, and I have no idea where I'm going, so I can't help but wonder if I just keep driving or do I stop and ask for directions at some cozy roadside gas station where people talk about the importance of helping other people and enjoying small-town life, and even the thought of it makes me want to laugh out loud, but to each their own, I think I will just keep driving straight until I can't anymore, or at least until I run out of gas and die on the side of the road, waiting for a paramedic with a beautiful smile to come and try to breathe life back into my body, and when I come back to life, wondering why she's wearing a yellow raincoat when it isn't even raining, or maybe it's a sundress, it's hard to tell because the filmstrip in my mind keeps slipping and jumping all over the white screen and I'm only able to piece together little things, and I have to admit I'm a little afraid of everything being fixed and seeing the film play perfectly on the screen and what it will look like or the person I will see, because I feel like I'm getting to know an entirely new person, someone I've never met before, or someone I knew a really long time ago who I've lost touch with and I just don't know if we'll have anything to talk about because there can't be anything we have in common anymore, one a recovering addict, the other, god only knows, and I can't say I'm interested in finding out, but apparently the recovering addict isn't such a bad person, at least that's what the nurses say when they come in to switch out my IV bag or ask if I need to be turned, and what I tell them is that I would really like to have the straps removed, but I'm told that isn't possible because it's hospital policy for people in my condition, a condition known as attempted suicide, but I wasn't trying to die, I was just trying to get really, really high one last time, but I guess taking half a bottle of pills is seen as an attempt to take your own life, not necessarily an attempt to get high, but no one knows what kind of tolerance a person has until they see it in action, and I'm sure if I was left on the sidewalk and the paramedics didn't see me as the one most likely to survive and spent more time on the woman in the yellow rain jacket on the street, they might have saved her and I would have woken up later that night and walked away half-naked down the street wondering if I had any more refills on that prescription, or if there were any more hits of acid to pass from my tongue to someone else's as we made love and then panic that the room was flooding or that traffic had suddenly stopped on the highway and what it meant for the drivers behind us or in front of us, worried that we might start up again and drive head-on into them, flying through the windshields, holding hands and kissing, breathing life into one another, and entering their cars on each side, one in yellow, the other half-naked, and someone inside the car wearing a sundress.

Most likely yellow as well.

Have you ever had suicidal tendencies in the past?

Does driving head-on into oncoming traffic count?

No.

Have you ever taken an excess of drugs with the intent to end your own life?

I always take an excess of drugs with the intent to end my own life.

No.

How long have you been a drug user?

I've been a drug user every day of my life because I live one day at a time.

I couldn't say.

Why do you abuse drugs?

I don't abuse drugs. I enjoy them.

I don't abuse drugs. I enjoy them.

Have you ever unintentionally overdosed?

There's no such thing as unintentionally overdosing. You take what you can handle and if you take more, it's because you want to die.

No.

What do you do for work?

I crash cars intentionally and collect the remains of people's broken lives.

I'm a tow truck assistant.

Do you have any family?

I don't remember. They are from a past I can't recall and don't care enough to dig for.

Probably.

Do you have anyone you can turn to?

Yellow dresses and raincoats.

No.

What will you do when you get out of here?

Live a clean and sober life, meet a beautiful woman with a perfect smile, get married, buy a house in the suburbs, raise two children, get a dog, mow the lawn, host barbecues, drink no more than three beers in a week, have Friday night sex with my wife, drive my kids to school, take up golf, commute to work, take lunch breaks, call meetings, wear ties, floss, eat a balanced breakfast, buy apples, read Newsweek, take vitamins, buy life insurance, set up a savings plan, retire, die.

Become a real person.

Are you worried you'll relapse?

Why? Because every single part of my body is screaming for something, anything, to make this interview feel less like a colonoscopy and give me the courage to get behind the wheel of some old, beat up car from Trevor's impound lot and cruise the highway looking for a golden nugget I can crash into and hope for death but be brought back to life by a kiss that breathes life back into my body, because that's the only real way to live, isn't it? You haven't lived until you've nearly died.

No.

What's the first thing you will do when you get released?

I will find the nearest drug dealer, spend the money I steal from your wallet after I stab you in the throat with your pen on the most potent, life-threatening drugs I can buy, then I'll get behind the wheel of a car and drive as fast as I can until I find just the right moment, a gap in the oncoming lane and I'll drive up the wrong way of an off-ramp and slam into the first car coming down and fly through the windshield and not even care if there are any yellow dresses.

Leave the city.

I met myself in a hospital room on the city's east side.

He's a bit of an asshole.

So what do I do now?

I
MET
YOU

on the highway off-ramp leading into the city. Or out of the city. In that moment when our headlights crossed, mine briefly illuminating your face before yours blinded me and then the two coming together, your smile gone in a flash of light, I remember thinking that I hoped we would meet.

I don't remember much about the immediate moments after. Just the smell of gasoline, the bitter taste of blood, and a pain on the top of my shoulder. You thought it was from a piece of flying glass but it was actually from the seatbelt digging into my skin when I was pushed toward the exploding airbag. I think that's what cut my lip. I remember the blood and I remember you wouldn't shut up about car accidents and bodies mangled in twisted metal wrecks but I was thankful for the distraction.

I knew I needed to be as far away from there as possible, so I went with you and that driver, Trevor, to the impound lot. You passed out in the front seat and Trevor said there was a couch in the break room that I was welcome to sleep on until I could call someone to come get me. I didn't tell him that I had no one to call, or no one I wanted to call. So I just stayed in the truck, your head on my shoulder, your hair sticky with my blood, and I remember thinking that it was all your fault. I think I even said it to you, but I can't remember for sure. I just needed someone to blame because I couldn't handle blaming myself anymore.

I left you there in the truck and climbed up onto the back and got in the car. The keys were still in the ignition and there was one of those stupid pine-tree air fresheners hanging from the rear-view mirror but it didn't give off any scent anymore. It felt familiar, but cars are so similar that you could sit in any car and recall some kind of memory. There's really nothing special about cars at all, even though we spend so much time in them, going back and forth to work or picking up kids from school or just driving to feel like we are going somewhere.

The lid of the centre console was open. I pulled out one of the cassette tapes and put it into the deck, but it didn't work. I looked through the rest of the tapes and the owner's manual, and there at the bottom was a piece of paper with an address, a weekly schedule, and a name written in pencil. It looked like something you would see on the backs of faded photographs in albums forgotten in drawers. I put it back in the console and tried to forget but my memory clung to the familiar smell of peppermint candies still in wrappers.

I thought about going to the hospital to see how you were. I read in the paper that two people were seriously injured the second time two cars met on an off-ramp that night, but they were in the same car. The passenger in the other car was sent to hospital with non-life-threatening injuries, so at least you didn't have to worry about your life being threatened. The woman driver fled the scene, the paper said. She did. She fled before the dust from the road and the shattered plastic had even settled onto the pavement though what the paper didn't say was that it was a man found in the driver seat. Well done.

I ran back down the off-ramp to the highway and just kept walking as though I was out for an evening stroll in one of the most dangerous places you could be until someone stopped and asked if I needed a ride. After I got in I saw the emergency lights coming at us in the distance and the driver, a young man, said there must have been a bad accident somewhere.

Maybe, I said.

I hope no one got hurt, he said.

I'm sure everyone's fine.

It's those goddamn drunk drivers. This is such a terrible time of day to be on the road. The sun isn't quite up yet and the drunks are all driving home while the early risers are heading into work. It's a recipe for disaster.

I couldn't listen to this again so I asked the driver to please be quiet. We listened to the tires mark the imperfections in the pavement and stared ahead at the distant taillights that seemed to stand still and the passing headlights blinking by one at a time. Seeing the bag on my lap, he asked me if I was leaving town. I told him I was and he said he was only going as far as a neighbourhood on the north side of the city and if I wanted he could drop me off at a bus station. I told him to just take me as far as he could and I would find another ride.

The driver tried to make small talk, telling me all about his midnight shift at a convenience store on the city's south side. He's been robbed three times this month, he said. The store has a policy not to resist and just hand over whatever's in the cash register and hope the crook goes away.

No amount of money is worth your life, right? The driver asked me.

No, I guess not. How much?

What?

How much money do they get?

It depends on the night, I suppose. Sometimes just fifty bucks, other times it could be three hundred. It all depends on how many smokes and chips and bottles of malt liquor we sell.

I asked him if he ever thought about pocketing the money and telling the manager he was robbed. I don't think the thought has ever entered his mind because he just shook his head as though I suggested he shoot the manager and take his money too. But maybe he's thinking about it now after I put the idea in his head. I hope so. I like to give people new ideas.

The sun was up by the time we got to his apartment. When I got out of the car he noticed the blood on my dress and the bandage on my shoulder and he asked me if I was okay. I assured him I was fine and thanked him for the ride, but he offered me something to wear or to try and clean my dress.

My girlfriend has already left for work, I'm sure she has something in the closet you could wear.

Good people intrigue me. It's like they don't know what they are doing or why. They just do things because they think it's the right thing to do. So I followed him inside.

The driver's girlfriend doesn't have a very extensive wardrobe, but he managed to find me an old navy blue dress with white dots. I asked him if there was anything with a little more colour, but he said he didn't want to take any of her new clothes or she'd kill him. I looked over his shoulder into the closet and noticed several brightly coloured dresses, not yellow though.

Are you sure she won't mind? I asked, slipping on the navy blue dress while he waited outside of the bedroom.

No, it's fine. She will understand. Should I throw your other dress in the laundry?

I handed him the dress through a crack in the door and thanked him for everything he'd done. After he walked away, I went back to the closet and pulled down a bright orange summer dress and held it to my body in the mirror. The driver's girlfriend must have lost weight between the time she bought the navy blue dress with white dots and the orange one. I knew it would be tight, but it would fit.

I was about to unzip the little bag to put the dress in when the driver called to me. So I left the dress on the bed and went out to the kitchen where he said he was making coffee and asked if I would like some. I told him I avoid stimulants and he offered tea, but I said water would be fine.

It will be a few minutes for the wash, he said. May I ask what happened?

I was in a car accident, I said.

Were you hurt?

I pointed to my shoulder and said just a small cut. Then he went on to tell me about a time when he was a child and the car he was in with his mom and dad rolled into a ditch after another car clipped the side when it crossed the centre line on a highway leading out of the city and how everyone was just hanging upside down held in place by their seatbelts.

I can't even describe what that feeling was like, but I know I'll never forget it, he said.

Some things are good to remember and forget at the same time, I told him.

Whose fault was it?

What?

The accident? Who was at fault?

I didn't answer right away because I was worried that maybe the driver had seen the accident and saw me running down the off-ramp and he was trying to figure out if I had done it intentionally. So I just told him I couldn't remember.

Did you leave the scene?

Are you interrogating me?

The driver apologized and said he didn't mean to offend me, he was just curious. Then he told me about how important it is to be there for the ones you love and while he was hanging upside down, he remembered how much his mother helped keep him calm by laughing the whole time and saying how funny it was that they were all hanging upside down together as a family. I don't know where I would be without her, he said.

Do you have a mother?

Do I have a mother? Is that what you're asking me?

Are you close?

We were.

So you're daddy's little girl?

Excuse me?

The driver tried to remember some saying he heard once about how when a child is married, a mother never loses a son and gains a daughter, meanwhile a father has to give away a bride but no father ever wants to, or something like that.

My father and I are really close, or we were, he said.

Then he grabbed the phone off the hook and said I could call my parents if I'd like, in case they are worried.

I told him that wasn't necessary.

You know what I remember most about that day? Besides my mother laughing and my father trying to hide his pain. Hanging there upside down, I remember seeing a woman walking away down the highway, like nothing was happening. Like she didn't have a care in the world. That's when I started to laugh. I'll never forget that. Or the dress she was wearing.

I decided that I had had enough questions and stories and I asked the driver to get my dress. He said he just put it in but I said I didn't care and I unzipped the navy blue dress with white dots and pulled it down and stood there in his kitchen in my underwear. The phone still in his hand started to beep but I don't think he heard it.

Just get my fucking dress, I said and he hung up the phone and put his hands up and told me to calm down and went to the laundry room. Water was dripping from the dress all the way down the hall and he threw it to me and the warm water sprinkled my bare skin. The blood stains were still there and looked bigger on the soaking wet fabric. I pulled the dress on over my head and turned around and asked if he would zip me up. He didn't hesitate. Some people do things just because they know it's the right thing to do.

I thanked him for the ride and got the bag from the bedroom and made my way for the door. But before I could leave, the driver called to me and said I should be more careful on the roads and try to avoid driving in the wrong lane.

I walked away from the apartment as fast as I could, water still dripping from my dress onto the sidewalk. People that I passed stared at me, trying to figure out how only my clothes seemed to be wet but the rest of my body was dry. I wanted to get back to the highway, to get into another car and tell the driver to drive as fast as they could and not to worry about veering off into the lane of oncoming cars.

I wish I could tell you why I did what I did, but the truth is, I'm not even sure and I've been asking myself that same question over and over again but never coming up with an answer. We try to tell ourselves that everything happens for a reason or that everything will work out in the end, but those are just lies we tell ourselves to make it feel like we have some sort of control over our lives. Losing control is the only truth we will ever know.

And that's why you do what you do, isn't it? You don't want to be in control because you don't want to live a lie. Maybe that's too easy. I don't even know you.

I went to see you in the hospital. You didn't know that though. Rather than finding my way back to the highway, I went further into the city and asked people for change for the bus. My dress was still damp and wrinkled and the blood stains were still there, so people felt sorry for me, I think, and it made it easy to get enough money. Some people even offered me rides, but I decided against that because I didn't want to end up back in someone else's apartment waiting for my dress to be washed and accused of purposefully driving a car head-on into another one.

At the hospital I didn't know who to ask for, so I asked the receptionist if there was a car accident victim admitted last night. There were several. I had no idea there were so many accidents on a given night. It really puts things into perspective knowing I'm not the only one out there causing mayhem and havoc on city streets.

The receptionist asked if I was okay, seeing the wrinkled blood stains on my dress and the bandage on my shoulder. I told him I was fine and that I was getting tired of people constantly asking me that.

So I ended up just walking up and down the hospital hallways. Each floor, each wing, until I saw Trevor. He was walking down a hallway with his hands in his jacket pockets and it looked like he was holding something. He noticed me and recognized me by my yellow dress.

I told him I was looking for you and he pointed back down the hallway to where you were. But before I could go, he asked me what happened.

We were in a car accident, remember? You picked us up.

No, not that, Trevor said. I mean what happened after that?

I don't know what you're talking about, I said, and tried to walk past, but he grabbed my arm. When he did, an IV bag fell out of his pocket and spilled across the hallway floor.

Trevor swore under his breath and he pulled me away from the puddle of painkillers spreading across the linoleum floor and told me I could have killed you.

Maybe he could have killed me, I said, and pulled my arm free from Trevor's hand and he told me the police were on their way.

You better hope they don't believe him when he says he wasn't driving.

Don't forget your medicine, I said, before walking away.

You were lying in the hospital bed. Your eyes were closed but I wasn't sure if you were dreaming. I'm not sure why I went there, why I wanted to see you. Maybe it was some strange sense of guilt, or like I owed you something. Maybe it was love. Wouldn't that be wonderful?

I should have opened the door all the way and sat next to you on the bed and told you I was sorry and then waited for your apology, but I don't think you have anything to apologize for. This was all my fault. Everything is my fault.

So instead I walked away, leaving you there with the cuts on your face and whatever other injuries were hidden under the hospital gown and bed sheets.

As I walked out of the elevator, a paramedic walked past me, turned, and told me how much she liked my dress. I thanked her and left the hospital and walked back to the highway and waited for a car to slow down and stop.

I managed to get rides but never out of the city. I hitched rides from truckers who took me as far as loading docks, minivans full of teenagers that brought me to clubs downtown. A family of five even stopped to offer me a ride. Whenever anyone asked where I was going I just said as far away from here as possible, but no one was travelling very far at all. It was like there was some gravitational pull keeping cars in orbit around the city and never letting any break away. After the initial conversations about where I was going and why, which were usually met by my silence, I could tell the people were silently trying to figure out what I was running from.

The funny thing was, I was trying to figure out the same thing from the passenger seat. Once you start running, the very moment you put one foot in front of the other or push down on the gas pedal, you stop thinking about what you're running from and only think about continually moving forward. And that's the goal, right? Otherwise we would just stay still with our thoughts and memories and glaring looks and judgmental accusations and the unbearable idea that we've somehow failed everyone around us. And the further we go the more things we can find to keep running from. So what, I was in two car accidents in the same night. So maybe I did have things to be running from and still do.

And it wasn't the fact that I left you there in the car, even pulling you over to the driver's seat to make it look like you were the one who was driving. I'm sorry for that by the way.

I wasn't running from the first accident either. The truth is, I was running long before any of that even happened. I was running before I stole a set of keys in the middle of the night, before I got in a car that didn't belong to me but felt all too familiar, with bags in the trunk that weren't mine, and long before our headlights touched.

So when the last ride finally dropped me off in some neighbourhood I had never been to before, with nothing but my stained and wrinkled yellow sundress and the bag I took from the trunk of the car, I didn't know what to do, where to go from here, how to keep running.

Sometimes I wish anytime we are going somewhere we could get into a car accident to make us stop and think about just what it is we are doing with our lives. I'm not sure if that worked for you. You had two chances to stop and think that night.

I have nowhere to go and no place to be. There are fewer highways here and even less off-ramps. I just need to find a car. Maybe someone will let me borrow one. Or maybe I can just steal one. I only need it for a short time. It won't take long. I just need to get in, start driving, and wait for a gap in the traffic and then start driving the wrong way again.

Maybe I'll meet you again somewhere down the road.

I
MEET
VICTORIA

in a church basement on the west side of the city, the same one my
parents were married in thirty-five years ago. At least I think. I
know it was some church in some part of the city that looked just
like this. I don't remember seeing any photographs hanging on
the wall of them on church steps holding each other and smiling
and feeling like it was the first day of the rest of their lives, because
the last day of their marriage was also the first day of the rest of
their lives.

I walk into the church basement with the same address as the
one on the piece of paper Shaw left on the hospital table, on one of
the days listed in the schedule written just below, and I'm really not
surprised it is a group counselling session for recovering addicts
because they are always held in church basements and I look around
the room half expecting to see everyone wearing yellow sundresses
or at the very least Shaw sitting there in a yellow raincoat sharing
her experiences about being addicted to killing pain with painkillers and how freeing it felt to run out into traffic wearing nothing
but that raincoat, but those are not the types of stories people share,
not that I know what stories people do share as this is the first time
I've ever been to a recovery program because I never considered actually
recovering since I never thought of myself as needing to recover
from anything, recovery means there was damage before, but if you
like what you see when you look in the mirror, if you can't see any
damage, there's nothing to recover from, so I don't know why my body
is completely free of any alphazolam, diazepam, methamphetamine,
benzodiaphines, psilocybin, lysergic acid diethylamide, and not even
a drop of alcohol in more than two weeks, and now I feel every

single little ache and pain, and all the car accidents have caught up with me and if I think hard enough I can pinpoint each pain to a night when I turned before I should have, or drifted over the centre line a little, or just straight-up rammed into the back of a car, and I can hear my big toe click from sideswiping a pickup truck when my foot got caught under the brake pedal trying to get out and run before the police arrived on the scene, or the ache in my shoulder from the time I was rear-ended when I slammed on the brakes in the middle of the highway and was thrown into the dash, and the stiffness in my neck from years and years of whiplash, and why anyone would want to live this way, I will never know. But back to Victoria.

I sit and listen to the peoples' stories about how they have been sober for years and years, or days and days, or just hours and hours, whatever, it doesn't really matter to me because none of their sob stories are going to make my road to recovery any easier and when it comes to my time to share why I'm here, I want to say I'm only here because of a woman in a yellow sundress, but instead I say what's expected of me and that I've been clean and sober for two weeks and one day after I watched a woman, high on acid, run out into traffic and get hit by a car, and the only thing I really remember, because I was so fucking high at the time, was the yellow dress she was wearing, and then I overdosed, but I made the decision to get clean before overdosing, and everyone looks at me like I'm a fucking bug in a jar and who are they to judge me?

The man running the group thanks me for sharing and then turns to a woman sitting directly across from me and asks her to share her story, and if not for the blue jeans, black tank top, and leather jacket I would swear I've seen her before in a flash of light, and when she stands to introduce herself I thought her name was Lola but she says its Victoria and that she is a recovering alcoholic who used to drink a bottle of scotch a day, a habit she developed after college to deal with the inadequacies of a liberal arts degree and wanting nothing more than to fit in with the culture of drinking and genetic predispositions that persisted in her family for generations and spilled out into her social life like a knocked over highball glass on a bar table rocked off balance by a man and a woman who can't keep their hands off one another and don't want to wait until getting home or even to the car, because they want everyone in the bar, everyone in the world to know how much they love each other, even if they don't really love each other, they just love the idea of loving someone and showing it off like pictures of their future children they keep in wallets and purses and shove in other people's faces hoping that someone actually cares that the little boy has his eyes or her nose or whatever other stupid facial feature that isn't even fully developed yet. But things got really bad after her mother died.

Victoria is asked how long it's been since her last drink and she says it's been one year, three months, and two days and she's been in three car accidents but doesn't mention that two of them came just weeks ago when she was already sober, and she only gave up drinking after her father got sick, and everyone applauds like that's some kind of big accomplishment and I guess it is, I'm really not an expert at this whole clean living thing and maybe it's something you have to celebrate every chance you get, and then Victoria says how she thinks about having a drink every day, and she's told that's normal, but she says no, it's not normal, because it's the only thing she thinks about every day and I want to speak up and say if it's the only thing she thinks about, then why doesn't she just drink and get it off her mind, because when you are constantly stoned or drunk you never have to think about when your next hit or drink is going to come from, but who am I to say anything about anyone else's recovery. As I said, this is all new to me.

When the meeting is over and everyone stands around and shakes each others' hands and talks about how long it's been since they injected, snorted, inhaled, swallowed something that made them feel far better than they feel now, I follow Victoria, who avoids this whole social aspect of recovery, and catch up to her on the basement steps leading into the narrow church hall and I ask her if she used a fake name, too, but she ignores me and keeps walking away, so I run after her and ask if she remembers me, which is greeted by a middle finger held up over her shoulder, so I ask her what it's like to think about something every day that she knows she can't have, and she stops but must think I'm joking, because she just rolls her eyes and starts to walk away again, so I try to be clearer and tell her that I'm just curious, because since I've been clean, the only thing I think about is what it would be like to be in a car accident while completely sober, and I say this because I think she might be the only person who would understand since she's been there before, we've been there before, and even if it is like an addiction, I tell her that thinking about it isn't so bad because at least it's something to focus on because what else is there really, and she thinks I'm joking again and we really aren't getting off on the right foot again, so I ask her if she has a happy and fulfilling life, and she walks up to me and leans in close and tells me to fuck off and mind my own goddamn business. I tell her that's not what I meant.

She asks me what I do mean and I tell her that I miss the numbness that comes with intoxication and not being in control and not thinking about it, because, I tell her, I'm just like you, there are things I think about every day so I know I'll remember but I'm afraid with my new found sobriety I'll forget, and since you've been thinking about it for one year, three months, and two days, I was hoping you could offer me a little advice on how you do it, and she knows I'm not joking this time, and she steps away and tells me she has to look after her own shit and can't be burdened with mine too, because all these new addicts come into these group sessions thinking the others who have scraped by this long will take them under their wings and lead them to the path of sobriety, when in reality, everyone is hanging on by a thread and just taking it one day at a fucking time and they should find their own way to deal with the shit in their lives and not put it on everyone else's shoulders, but I tell her she has me all wrong and that I'm not looking for her to help me with my sobriety, I just want to know why she does it, and this doesn't sit well either, because she asks me what makes me think it's any business of mine. Because we've met before, I say, and I hold up the crumpled piece of scrap paper and I can see by the way she looks at it that she is starting to remember.

Victoria agrees to hear me out, so I suggest we go somewhere to talk and I ask if she has a car, which she does, and we start to drive, the streets mostly empty now because it's after eleven and everyone else in the city is either thinking about scoring, already high, or not aware that that is a part of life, and I tell Victoria this, that we are actually the special ones, because we are somewhere in between what is normal and abnormal, we are abnormal people trying to become normal people, but there's no real way to reach that goal, because as she said, our minds will always be thinking about something else, no matter where or what we are doing, even on our wedding day we will be thinking of how fucking amazing it would be to be shit-faced right now, or how at our mother's funeral we will only think about being completely and utterly stoned out of our minds to numb whatever it is normal people feel at funerals, or on our child's first day of school we will wish they would just get on the fucking bus already so we can sneak away into the backyard and shove so much cocaine up our nose that it will bleed and we will be found when the bus comes back at the end of the day and there's no one there to greet the child and the bus driver calls the police. Victoria stops me and tells me I'm getting a little off track.

What I'm trying to say, I tell her, is it's okay to think about it all day, everyday, because it's just who you are and you should embrace that, because there's nothing worse than denying who you are, you'll never get to normal, and you don't have to be abnormal, so just be you, but then she interrupts me and tells me to just stop talking because she knows what I'm trying to do, even though I don't even know what I'm trying to do, but apparently I'm full of shit and just trying to get her to give in to her thoughts because that's what I want to do and I don't want to be alone, just like all the pathetic new addicts who come to these group meetings and see some fine piece of ass, wanting to take advantage of someone they think is in a vulnerable position and take her to some lame ass party, get her drunk or stoned, and fuck her all night and then move on to the next one after she totally fucks up her life one last time and gives in to the thoughts all together until they completely take over and become the last thing she ever thinks about until the moment she dies. I tell her she could not be more wrong.

We are on the highway when she thinks she's figured everything out and she pulls over onto the shoulder and tells me to get the fuck out of her car because she's not playing any of my games and she doesn't care if we are on the highway and there's a very good possibility that I could be hit by a speeding car that is driving faster than its headlights and won't see me in time to swerve into oncoming traffic and avert a disaster by causing another, much more serious one, so I get out of the car but before she can pull back into the lane I'm illuminated by the headlights with my hands on the hood feeling the vibration from the engine, and I yell to her that I don't have any of the thoughts she does, and everything she said isn't true, aside from maybe the fucking all night part, but I've never been one to do that when I'm sober anyway, because it's easier pretending to love someone when you don't feel anything, physically or emotionally, and she opens the door and tells me to get the fuck out of the way because she's not going to fuck me and I say that's fine, we don't have to do that, and I ask her what she's thinking about right now and she closes the door and looks up and down the highway, then leans against the car and says that I already know what she's thinking about, so I walk over to her, put my hands on her shoulders, but not in an intimate way, though I try to lift up the collar of her leather jacket with my thumb to see the cut on her shoulder, but she cocks her head at me so I stop and tell her I want to show her how to not think about it all day, every day, and she doesn't say anything more, so I open the door and she asks where we're going. It's not far, I say, and I offer to drive.

We keep driving down the highway, the few cars still out passing by, their headlights flashing across our faces and the street lights above pulsing like a drug addict's heart, and Victoria asks me again where we are going, and I let the car drift a little over the centre line, which she doesn't notice at first, so I let it go a little further, and she doesn't say anything until another car appears in the opposite lane and has to swerve around us and she asks me what the hell I'm doing, so I apologize and bring the car back into our lane, and she asks me if I'm trying to be funny or playing some kind of sick joke, and I tell her I just wasn't paying attention for a moment, and I ask her what she misses most about drinking, and she tells me it's none of my business and she doesn't like talking about it anyway, so instead I tell her about what I miss most about it, and about the numbness, and of not caring, and not being a real person, and I seem to have caught her attention, because she says she never felt like a real person either, and tell I her she's not, or wasn't, and that it's really not such a bad thing, and as I explain this, I let the car drift a little further over the centre line and she tells me to watch where I'm going, so I apologize again and tell her about how the first time I ever did drugs was the best day of my life, like I was being reborn, and even though I don't remember the exact time or the circumstances, I knew it was an important time in my life, like everything before had been erased or never even happened, and Victoria tells me that no one ever thinks that, let alone a recovering addict, but I'm not a recovering addict because I wasn't broken before, and she wants to know why I stopped, and I tell her she already knows why and I talk about yellow sundresses and headlights, raincoats and heavy traffic, car accidents and tow trucks, hospital gowns and IV bags, and say that the only way for me to know if you are real or not, was to get clean, and see if I could find you again. Where is your dress?

I find a gap in traffic on the highway just in time for an off-ramp coming up and I swerve and cross the four lanes and start going up in the wrong direction, and Victoria is screaming and reaching for the wheel, but we keep going up the ramp, and I wait for the headlights of a car coming down the ramp, lighting up my face until coming into contact with mine and turning everything dark, and seeing only yellow as the metal twists and bends on impact, but I just keep driving and see nothing, not one car, even at the top of the ramp and in all four lanes on the highway heading in the other direction, so I let off the gas and the car slowly comes to a stop on the empty highway, and Victoria gets out of the car and starts screaming again, calling me a psycho, and a freak, and how it was all my fault, and how I could have killed us, and I see, as she waves her arms in all directions, pointing back to the off-ramp and the headlights off in the distance down the highway, that she isn't wearing a dress at all, just blue jeans and a black tank top under a leather jacket, and I'm still trying to process everything that just happened and whether or not I am very lucky or very unlucky, I'm not sure which, but Victoria says we are the luckiest people on earth to not be dead right now, so I roll down the window and tell her that's how easy it is to forget, and ask her if she's thinking about getting a drink, and she stops screaming at me. I wasn't, she says, but I am now.

Victoria orders a double scotch. I drove us to a bar on the city's east side after she got back in the car on the highway. The first thing she said when she got back in was take me to a bar. So I did and here we are. The waiter brings the drink and places it in front of Victoria. She doesn't pick it up or even look at it, instead she just looks at me and asks me if I've ever done anything like that before.

I can't remember, I say. But I have been in a few accidents in the past.

What if there had been another car?

What if there had been?

Victoria looks down at her drink and says she's never wanted a drink more in her entire life so I tell her to drink it.

You really want me to fail, don't you?

I tell her that it doesn't matter what she does and I think this upsets her because she looks away. I think she wants to cry and I don't blame her. Maybe this is the first time anyone has ever been completely honest with her. It's easier to lie to people who don't want to hear the truth, but these are the people who need to hear it the most.

Victoria tells me she decided to get sober the day after her father's cancer diagnosis. The decision took time and the second time he entered the hospital was the day she had her last drink. It was the only way she could go there and face what was happening. I liked not fully being aware that he was dying, she says, because I was thinking about something else.

Is it like being numb? I ask.

No, it wasn't about being numb, she says. It was about not being fully present, like only my body was there but my mind wasn't because it only thought about where I would get my next drink, the feeling of it hitting my lips and warming my tongue, what it would feel like to be drunk again, just this constant little voice in my head talking over what the doctors were saying, what my sister was saying, what everyone was saying about what was happening to my father. That little voice got me through that.

Wouldn't having an actual drink make it just as easy? I ask.

It wouldn't have worked, she says. I had been an alcoholic for fourteen years before that. It would have just been like any other day. I was numb after my mother died, but it didn't take away any of the pain. I needed something different. And that turned out to be sobriety.

And what happened after he died?

He's still alive, Victoria says. The cancer keeps coming back, so I have to keep listening to the little voice asking me when I'll get that next drink. I keep telling myself that I can drink again after he's dead. Can you imagine anything more horrible? The voice went quiet when you crossed the highway and I realized just how much I've come to depend on it. It's like a new kind of addiction, and I wonder if it will ever go away, either by drinking again or just with time, if another voice will take over, asking me if I'll ever hear the first one again. Sometimes we come to depend on our own self-doubt and obsessions and addictions so much that we don't know if we will recognize ourselves after they're gone. I don't know what's harder, giving in or thinking about giving in.

I reach across the table and drink the scotch, even though scotch has never been my drink of choice. Victoria thanks me and asks me about the woman in the yellow dress.

I'm not even sure if I remember anymore.

Some things are easy to forget. Do you think she's out there?

I'm not sure. I guess I'll just have to try again.

I leave the booth with the empty glass and Victoria listening to the little voice in her head. She's too distracted and doesn't realize I still have the keys.

I met Lola in a church basement, but it wasn't Lola, it was Victoria, who wasn't using a fake name, and then I stole her car and started driving down the highway in the middle of the night after buying her a drink at a bar on the one year, two month, and third day anniversary of her sobriety, and I guess you could say it's also the day I broke my own sobriety of two weeks, and then I just left her in that bar with the voices in her head and the other drunks at the bar and in the booths who don't see themselves as drunks, but call themselves other names, like social drinkers, partygoers, unwinders, and whatever other lie they want to tell themselves to help them get through the night and then into their cars where they will drive home after drinking shots of whisky or

tequila or slamming pints of the latest craft beer and thinking they
are sophisticated because they can detect how many hops are being
used and all that bullshit people tell themselves and tell others in
bars, and I will admit that I feel a little guilty for leaving Victoria
there and stealing her car with every intention of crashing it head-
on into the next vehicle I can find on the highway just in the hopes
that I can put everything to rest and not worry about the woman
in the yellow dress who I can't help but see in every car I pass and
kick myself for missing my opportunity to swerve in front of it just
so I can see her again, and I almost start to laugh, because this
woman and her dress has become like a voice in my head, just like
Victoria has to listen to the constant questions of where she will
get her next drink, like a new addiction to help her get through
things like cancer and family, I have to see if there are any yellow
dresses on the highways and off-ramps, for no other reason than to
see if she is there, if she is real, and not just a dream I had, a cul-
mination of all my attempts to crash cars and survive, to steal petty
things, and just keep going another day, and it's about more than
just finding out if she's real, but finding out why she did it, so I
keep driving, drifting over the centre line, and there are plenty of
gaps tonight, so I drive up off-ramps and down on-ramps, sometimes in the right direction, sometimes not, until I lose count and
I'm always greeted by nothing, but then just as I turn onto another
one, I look out the passenger side and see another car drive across
four lanes of traffic in the other direction, and go up the opposite
ramp and I watch it until the lights round the corner and disappear
and when I look forward again I'm greeted by the familiar sight of
headlights, but I'm too late, I can't see the driver behind the wheel
because the lights are already out.

I
MEET
VICTORIA

in the hospital on the city's east side, the same hospital I was taken to to be treated for a hyperextended knee and broken ribs and cuts to my face when a woman in a yellow sundress holding a bag in her lap crossed four lanes of traffic and drove the wrong way up an off-ramp leading into the city, but this time things feel different, because when I wake up, and Victoria is there, I still feel numb from whatever cocktail of meds are being pumped into my blood from the IV hanging next to the bed, but I feel more than numb, I feel empty, completely drained, like I really, truly am just a body with a mind floating outside of it, but seeing Victoria sitting there in the corner, looking out the window at the purple morning light that few people get to see on a regular basis, I feel grounded, like everything is being forced and pushed back down into my body on the hospital bed, it's really not so terrible because it gives me a presence of mind that maybe being present isn't such a bad thing, and when she notices I'm awake, I come together a little more, and she tells me she never reported the car stolen, she never said the person she lent it to was leaving from a bar, and the person who had the keys was mentally disturbed and talked about ending his own life, and that was actually really thoughtful of her to do, even though I haven't seen any police yet coming to question me about my third accident in the last month, two of which they actually know about, and the second one where I was behind the wheel, and I ask Victoria about the other car, and she tells me the driver was killed, a twenty-year-old man on his way to start his night shift at a convenience store on the city's north side, but it turns out he was hopped up on stimulants to keep him sharp for when punks and petty criminals walk through the front door of the store and demand cash and smokes and bottles of malt liquor while waving a knife or a baseball bat or a crowbar in his face, and because the cars spun around more than once, the police determined the convenience store clerk was the one driving the wrong way up the off-ramp, even though that would have put him driving away from his job in the city's north side, but his girlfriend told the police that he had been thinking about quitting his job for weeks because he was tired of being away from her all the time, though a distance had grown between them after she came home one day and found her favourite navy-blue dress with white dots lying on the kitchen floor, and her orange dress on the bedroom floor, and she believed he had either been inviting women over to the apartment during the day to try on her clothes and pretend to be her, which was flattering in at least some way, or much less flattering, he was dressing up in her clothes in an attempt to be her, but that's when the fighting started, and it continued throughout the day when he should be sleeping, so he started using uppers, caffeine pills, and cocaine to keep him awake and ready for robbers during the midnight shift, and when he left late that night, he didn't say he was sorry, he didn't try to offer any kind of explanation, and he didn't tell her he loved her, only that he would be back in the morning, unless, of course, this was the night he finally quit his job, but he didn't get there to even try, because instead, as he was driving to work down the highway, he thought he spotted an orange car he recognized driving in the opposite direction, so he took the first off-ramp he could find, and then a second, and a third to start going in her direction, and he was going in so many different directions he could no longer keep track, and that's when he met me, and I wonder if the driver of the other car was wearing a yellow sundress, because there's no way to know for sure, but he didn't find her and neither did I, and I ask Victoria if there were any other car accidents that night, and she shrugs her shoulders and says she doesn't know, none that she's heard of anyway, so whoever was driving that other car must have made it up the ramp and stopped in the middle of the highway and maybe someone was outside of the car screaming at her about how she could have killed them both, and even though I'm numb and can't really feel anything, I can feel my heart break a little, so I tell Victoria that I'm really happy she's here and that I didn't want to be alone, even if being alone and being with someone isn't all that different for me, and not for her, because she has the voice in her head constantly whispering to her about finding that next drink and I have nothing to listen to, no one to hear me and everything that spews from my brain or my mouth, and that's not such a bad thing because most of what I say and think isn't worth being listened to anyway, but Victoria sees this as an opportunity to stand up and sit on my bed and put her hand on my arm, just like a paramedic did once at the scene of an accident, and tell me that everything will be okay and that they are going to take good care of me, and then have sex with me right there in the twisted wreck of a car while wearing a yellow raincoat because it must be raining outside, making the roads slick and most likely explaining why the crash happened in the first place, but I like the feeling of having someone here, even if I can't feel it, and Victoria tells me that her father is upstairs dying of cancer for the third time this year, and she keeps telling herself that she can have a drink after he finally dies because she won't have the need to rely on any voices whispering in her head asking her when she will get that next drink, and sometimes she can't even help herself from screaming back that she'll have a drink after he's dead, but that never works, because addictions are persistent, they never go away or listen to reason, and I ask her if the voice is helping her through this, too, through me and my broken body, because, after all, she's here, sitting on the edge of my bed, holding my arm and telling me that everything will be okay, even if she hasn't actually said those words, and she tells me she wanted to see how I was doing and thank me again for drinking that scotch so she didn't have to before her father dies and she doesn't even care that I took her car and smashed it beyond recognition because it was a rental anyway and she needed the strength to be sober just a little while longer as she waits for the cancer to consume what's left of her father, and I ask her if it would be easier if I just let the internal bleeding drain the rest of my life now, or the swelling in my brain to keep pushing against my skull until I become even less of a real person, and whatever other injuries are slowly killing me to just finish the job, but she tells me she would prefer if I could hang on, at least as long as her father, and I think that's the closest I've ever come to someone telling me they love me, and there is a small part of me, very small, that almost wishes I wasn't so numb and could feel whatever feeling that comes with hearing someone say they wish I would stay alive long enough so they could avoid having a drink and facing the reality of life, because isn't that what true love really is?

I stay with Victoria after I'm released from the hospital. I'm given more prescription painkillers to numb the pain the doctors think I'm in from a shattered pelvis, a ruptured spleen, severe head trauma that may cause permanent damage, and a broken foot. Victoria even wheeled me out of the hospital in a wheelchair after I told her I had nowhere to go, but we were already at the elevator when I told her that.

She has a small apartment on the city's west side in an affluent neighbourhood adjacent to a park and across the street from a school. She says she likes listening to the kids yell and scream and laugh at recess because children remind her that the world isn't such a terrible place. Children never see the world for what it truly is. That only comes as we get older and realize how shitty those kids we once played tag with on the playground or found hiding in a cupboard during a game of hide-and-seek really are.

The doctors told me I would be looking at a very long recovery and will need weeks of physiotherapy and follow-up appointments, and maybe even surgery to completely make me whole again. Victoria said she will help me through it, even though the doctor quietly pulled her aside and whispered to her that she is taking on a lot of work, but she said that's fine, she needs something to distract herself from life. So what better way to do that than by trying to bring life back to someone else?

Our days are mostly spent with a regimented schedule of feeding me painkillers, turning me over so I don't get bedsores, doing exercises so my muscles don't forget their purpose, and then feeding me more painkillers. I tell Victoria that she's really good at this and she tells me she's a nurse in a retirement home.

So you watch people die every day, I say.

I prefer not to look at it that way, she says.

Is that why you drink?

I drank for a lot of reasons. That was probably one of them.

What was it like?

What was what like?

Being there.

Victoria tells me it's not as bad as everyone thinks. It's not like being in a building surrounded by hundreds of people on life support and ventilators, just waiting to die. Many seniors remain active, their minds no different from when they were in their twenties, it's just their bodies that are failing because nothing lasts forever.

But there are people dying? I ask.

Of course. People die every day. I suppose just more of them do in a retirement home. It's just a matter of numbers.

Were you close to them?

No, Victoria says. I sort of stopped seeing them as people. I just started to see chores. Feeding, changing, turning, cleaning, it was all just a schedule.

I think my laughing upsets her but I tell her that I feel like I've heard that before and I ask her if I'm just a routine, if she doesn't see a real person.

I see whatever you want me to see, she says.

That doesn't really answer my question, but I decide not to push the issue and just accept it for what it is.

Our routine continues for weeks. Sometimes she opens the window before she goes to work or to visit her dad in the hospital so I can listen to the children outside in the playground. I sometimes forgot children even existed because I so rarely saw them and when I did, it was when they were in the back seats of cars and crying after I drove my car into the back of a minivan or clipped the side of a sedan. As far as I know, no child has ever died in an accident I've been a part of, but children shouldn't be out on the road late at night anyway, as far as I'm concerned. There are too many dangerous drivers out there.

But that's one of the best parts about not being a real person. I'm not held to the same moral standards as everyone else. I don't feel guilt or shame or remorse. If I did I wouldn't do what I do. I would drive straight, never crossing the centre line and never brake too hard and never step on the gas. I would have a regular, nine-to-five job, and commute to work like a responsible adult and not think about what could be found in someone's trunk or back seat or not feel alive by almost dying. To me, that is like a dream, just like to others, I'm like a dream. Or a nightmare. Or something entirely worse that I haven't even thought of yet.

Don't judge me though. Unless you've lived even the tiniest bit of your life in my shoes or driven even the shortest of distances in my car, you have no way of knowing what it's like, which is why I'm trying to tell you. And I don't recommend it. Once you try it, you'll never stop. The voice in your head will always win. I don't even hear it anymore because I always just give in. I'm always one step ahead. Or several highway exits. It makes life easier.

I also may have lied earlier when I said I don't care whether I'm alone or not. When Victoria is gone, I feel lonely and I'm left to either lie in bed all day, or, if she helps me out of bed before she leaves, wheel around her small apartment and listen to laughter of children or watch terrible daytime TV that never holds my attention unless there is a news story about a massive ten-car pile-up on the highway.

So when she isn't there I pretend she is and I talk to her and I laugh at the jokes she never tells and I look through the books on her shelves, mostly romance novels and Stephen King, and the odd addict recovery manual or brochure that talk about not giving into temptation, seeking support from others, and the health risks that come with overconsumption.

I love how every expert who puts out a book tries to tell you something different. The tough love experts try to tell you that you are weak and that everything that has ever happened to you in your life is your fault, including your addiction. But that's not true at all. There are plenty of things that happen to us that we have no control over. No one decides to get cancer. No one wakes up one day and says I want to be a drunk or a junkie. No one thinks the oncoming car in the other lane will swerve in front of them.

Then there are the softer, sweeter experts, who try to tell you that nothing that has happened in your life is your fault because you are strong and just unlucky. You drink because your parents did or because they beat you. You do drugs because of an injury suffered three years ago during a car accident and then became addicted to prescription painkillers because overzealous doctors make money off the amount of pills they dole out just like common drug dealers on street corners. But this is a lie too because everything is a choice. We choose to start drinking as a way to hide the pain of a traumatic childhood. We choose to keep popping pills because we would rather be numb than face another second of pain. We choose to cross the centre line on the highway.

I say this as I take more painkillers from the bottle in the pocket of my robe and put the self-help books back and continue to roll around the apartment.

In Victoria's bedroom there are pictures on the wall of her and her father, pre-cancer because he doesn't look quite so empty. There are pictures of cottages on lakes and city skylines with Victoria stretching her arms out as if to say: look at this, look at where I am. She looked happy in her youth. This must have been before she started drinking. Maybe right at the beginning when it still seemed like a good idea and was fun and hadn't become an obligation, an escape, the only thing she thinks about.

I wheel around to the bedside table where there is another photograph. It's not in a frame, it's just leaning there against the lamp. It's a photograph of Victoria with her arm around another woman. The woman is wearing a yellow sundress and I think I've seen her face before. It was lit up by bright lights, and expressionless, like in the photo. Victoria is smiling.

I wonder how many pills I have left.

VICTORIA MEETS ME IN THE HOSPITAL ON THE CITY'S EAST SIDE, the same one I was taken to at least two other times that I can think of, or maybe it's three now, I can't really remember, and this time they had to pump my stomach of at least a dozen high-strength prescription painkillers and I throw up charcoal, which isn't an easy thing to do when you can barely turn your body to the side, so most of the black sludge from my stomach ends up on my chin and down the front of my hospital gown and Victoria wipes it up and tells me it's okay, to not be embarrassed or ashamed, and she doesn't really know anything about me, because I don't feel embarrassed or ashamed or anything even remotely resembling a real human emotion, and she tells me it's normal to accidentally take too many pills, and I cannot believe how much denial she is in, and I try to tell her this, but I don't think my words are coming out all that clearly, because she just ignores whatever I say, including that she is a stupid bitch who knows nothing about me and I took all the pills on purpose because I wanted to get clean again, and I try to ask about the woman in the yellow dress I saw in a car on the highway, or maybe she was standing in front of a tree wider than the two of them together, her smiling, and the woman expressionless, but she doesn't hear that either and I wonder if I've lost my ability to speak all together, because after all, the doctor did say I

could have permanent brain damage and maybe I dreamt everything, maybe I'm not even alive or near death and I'm a patient in the
retirement home where Victoria works and I'm just a routine for her,
a set of tasks she has to do to earn her pay cheque and go home to an
empty apartment and listen to the voice in her head telling her she can
drink when her father dies, the voice she relies on to even go see her
father now and not think about him dying, but she stays, she doesn't
move on to the next routine, so I can't be there yet, and she sits down
next to me, her fingers stained black, and tells me that she was just
upstairs to see her dad and that he's not doing so well, and that it's
really just a matter of time now, and even the voice in her head
screaming for her stupid ass to just walk down the street and down
highball after highball of top-shelf scotch isn't doing enough to shield
her from the situation and the feelings of loneliness and abandon-
ment, and I wonder if I'm partly to blame, that seeing me and caring
for me is just too much reality, too much pain and suffering for her
mind and that voice to handle, and I tell her to leave me alone and
never visit me again and to go down the street and drink so much
alcohol that the only thing that will save her is having her stomach
pumped and throwing up black tar, and maybe then she will see that
not being real isn't such a great existence after all, but first she has to
experience it, she has to cross the centre line again and again, but she
doesn't hear this either and I wonder if it's just my mouth that's not
working or my brain, and maybe I'm not even talking, maybe I'm only
thinking these things, or maybe I'm only dreaming this entire routine, but I can feel her hand on my arm again, and it makes things
come into focus and feel a little less unreal, even though she still tells
me I'm crazy, and stupid, and that if I don't actually try to get clean,
I'm going to die one of these days, and I tell her that's not such a bad
thing because when you live like I do, death is just a part of life and
somehow it has eluded me all these years and it doesn't seem to matter
what I do, I just can't die, and I like to think it's because I'm immortal
or that there is some greater purpose for me and it's just a matter of

time before I find it and when I fulfill whatever it is I have to do with my time on this earth, I will crash a car at ninety kilometres per hour into the front of a semi-truck and there will be no recognizing me after that, no saving me because there will be nothing left of my body for paramedics in yellow raincoats to save, but Victoria doesn't think the same way, because she says that life is precious and we shouldn't waste it and that she only really realized that when I turned the car across four lanes of highway traffic and drove the wrong way up an off-ramp, and she thought the entire time that she was going to die, and for the first time in a long time, she wanted to be alive, even if it meant watching her father die, because watching someone die or slowly killing ourselves one drink at a time makes us realize how lucky we are to be alive, and that's something she took for granted while working in a retirement home, she had become so numb to the end of life that it didn't seem like something she would ever have to experience, so now when she goes to work, she doesn't see things as a routine, she sees people lying on the beds, she sees names, histories, families, and she talks to them, she asks them how they are doing, she asks little old ladies to tell her stories about their grandchildren, she asks old men to tell her about what it was like serving in the army for forty years, and she asks women on ventilators if they've lived a happy life, even though they can't answer, and she asks men, whose faces are contorted in pain what she can do to make the last little bit of time they have on this earth a little more bearable, and by talking, allowing words to leave our lips in the face of death, the voices in our head get a little less loud, and now she asks me what she can do to help me from spiralling further and further down, her black fingers squeezing my forearm, and I say to her that she can tell me about the woman in the yellow dress in the photograph on her nightstand leaning against the lamp, the one where she's smiling and the woman isn't, the one that says, written on the back in pencil, me and Lola, Stanley Park, '92.

I ask her if she can hear me and she says she's been listening to me this entire time.

I
MET
YOU

on an off-ramp somewhere in the city, maybe even on the one running down from the highway near a laundromat where I met Sasha. She wrapped a towel around me after seeing me standing naked in front of a washing machine watching my yellow dress, bra, and underwear tumble around and around. I didn't even notice that other people were staring at me, including men who usually have to undress women with their minds, trying to hide erections in loose shorts they only wear on laundry day. I was someplace else, my mind travelling down long stretches of highway, my eyes blinded by headlights, and I was deafened by the sound of breaking glass and metal colliding with metal. Sasha came up to me just before the attendant did, to ask me to leave, which would have forced me to wear my soaking wet dress again, and listen to the water drip on the sidewalk.

Sasha told the attendant everything was fine and we just needed some space. She asked if I was okay and if I needed help, but I told her I'm just waiting for my clothes to be done.

You're hurt, she said, seeing the bandage on my shoulder and the other cuts and bruises that I wasn't even aware of. Were you in an accident?

One or two, I said, and kept staring at the clothes going up and down, the pink and yellow swirling around like distorted emergency lights.

Do you have any other clothes? Sasha asked.

I didn't answer but she noticed the little bag sitting on top of the dryer and reached for it, asking if there were any spare clothes inside, but I screamed at her not to touch it and I grabbed it off the machine and held it to my chest, the towel falling down and men leaning back to get another view and the attendant yelling to either cover up or get the hell out. I thought this bag would have been long gone by now, lost on the highway, or picked up by some fireman or paramedic or tow truck driver. That's what I wanted all along but now I can't let it out of my sight. It's strange, the things we choose to hold on to, the things we can't leave behind. Why is it easier to tell someone you never want to see them again than it is to just leave everything else behind on the road?

Sasha apologized, pulling the towel back up to cover my breasts and said she wasn't trying to take anything.

She offered me a shirt that was two sizes too big and jogging pants that hung off my waist that were already washed and dried. She held up the towel so I could put them on without anyone seeing. I've always found it strange how comfortable women are with other women's bodies. Until that day only a handful of people had ever seen me naked. I wasn't thinking about that when I pulled the yellow dress over my head and put it into the washing machine. Despite the eyes staring at me, I had never felt more alone than I did standing naked in that laundromat. But a woman standing naked in a laundromat with cuts and bruises on her body waiting for her only clothes to get clean is not like standing in the middle of the street and screaming for help where most respectable human beings will come running to ask what's wrong. There is something about the calmness of a naked woman in public that seems to garner both interest and disdain. Only other women who have found themselves in similar situations know that something is terribly wrong.

Has this ever happened to you? I asked Sasha.

Running out of clothes? No, not since high school anyway.

No, I meant standing naked in a laundromat.

No, Sasha said. It hasn't. But don't worry about it.

I wasn't worried about it. It didn't matter to me. I don't think I feel shame or guilt anymore, at least not like other people do. If any of the horny men, guided by their erections, had walked up to me, asked for my number or even grabbed a handful of my breasts, I think I would have just stared at my dress in the washing machine, wishing I had something sharp and as long as their dicks that I could stab into their chests, all the while wondering when I became so numb. But I thanked Sasha and I even hugged her and feeling the touch of another person, a woman, I wanted to cry. Maybe it was the hunger, or the cold from being naked, or feeling completely and totally lost in a city I didn't even want to be in, but for the first time in as long as I can remember, I felt vulnerable. I felt like I could shatter into a million pieces of broken glass on the highway that crunch under the boots of firefighters and paramedics. Or maybe it was just the kindness of Sasha, who knew nothing about me other than that I was naked, hurt, and didn't have anything to wear but a blood-stained yellow sundress.

We sat down and waited for our clothes to be done, ignoring the leering looks from the men who stayed long after their own laundry was done, expecting me to strip out of the baggy shirt and pants once my dress was dry, but Sasha just folded it up with my bra and underwear and placed it on the top of her dried clothes in the basket. Even though my clothes were done, I stayed and listened to Sasha talk as she folded the rest of her clothes, mostly small children's shirts and pants and tiny little socks.

Sasha told me all about her family — three kids and a husband who works twelve-hour shifts at an assembly plant. There's something about listening to a mother talk about her family that is so intoxicating. It's like listening to a junkie talk about getting high or a drunk talk about overcoming the urge to drink. It's a mixture of both pride and sorrow. She said she stays home with the kids most days and takes care of the house work. It's not easy work, she says, wrapping a little pink shirt around her hands before folding it and placing it in the basket. But someone has to do it, right? Pride and sorrow.

I could tell then that the reason she came up to me and wrapped a towel around my naked body was both an instinct as a mother, but also an opportunity to help someone who was worse off than her. And I didn't mind being that person, so when she asked me to tell her about my life, I just told her I had to get away for a while, get back on the road, drive, and I could tell that there were a lot of scenarios swirling around in her head, from an abusive boyfriend, to a death in the family, or maybe I had even committed some unspeakable crime and was on the run from the police. People always want to know but are always too afraid to ask.

When all her clothes were done, she didn't hold up the towel so I could change back into my dress. Instead she offered to take me home with her so she could iron it for me to get rid of all the wrinkles from letting it dry on me after leaving the driver's apartment when it was still wet. The blood stains were mostly gone though.

We drove in a small, orange, two-door car with a cracked windshield to a house two blocks away with a waist-high chain-link fence and very little grass. It smelled like cigarette smoke and fresh laundry and even though the curtains were open, there was somehow a lack of light inside. Sasha pulled an ironing board out from a little door in the wall and spread out my dress but before she started she offered to make me something to eat. I couldn't remember the last time I ate anything so I accepted the offer and she made me a bowl of soup and a grilled cheese sandwich and as I ate I watched the calming back and forth motion of her hand guiding the iron across my dress.

I was running a little toy car across the table with my finger, bumping it into the other cars left there, recalling and avoiding memories, when Sasha asked me if I had children. I shook my head and said I've never been very good with children.

No one is good with children, Sasha said. At least not right away. It's something you learn. Which I always found pretty funny because we were all children once. You would think we would just know what they want based on our own experiences. But then again, if we were given everything we wanted, we probably wouldn't have survived to adulthood.

Sasha laughed at her own joke, at least I assumed it was a joke, even though it was the truth. I've never been good with children because I've always felt you should just give them what they want, which would mean the extinction of the human race. I always got what I wanted and look what's left. I asked Sasha how old her children are and she told me she has a four-year-old, a six-year-old, and an eight-year-old. And a son from her first marriage who just turned eighteen. She was only seventeen when she had him.

I think it's better having at least more than one, she said, because that way the older ones help you raise the younger ones. I couldn't have done it without my oldest. He was a godsend.

I asked her what it was like being a mother at such a young age and she said it probably saved her life. I used to party all the time, go to clubs, snort coke, and get blackout drunk. That's just the life I knew. And then after one night getting it on in the back seat of a car with some guy I met at a club on the city's west side, we were pregnant. And he proposed to me and we were married and then living in a small, one-bedroom apartment on the city's north side. I told myself then and there in the doctor's office after finding out I was pregnant that I was going to give up that life of a stupid teenager and I did. A child shouldn't suffer because of choices he has no control over.

My husband, well, he didn't give up that life, at least not right away, and I was pretty much on my own right after the wedding. But he was only twenty-years-old at the time, so I don't know why I thought he would change. He didn't have anyone growing inside of him that depended on him more than anything. He only had me, but I don't think he realized how dependent I was on him. Men take a longer time to grow up. He did eventually. But that was a long time ago and a lot has changed. I married again and I'm very grateful for my husband now. But he could walk out the door tomorrow and I know we would be fine. I know my eldest, who I gave up everything for, would give up everything for me.

I asked Sasha what happened to her first husband. She set the iron down on the end of the flimsy board stuck to the wall and pursed her lips.

He died several years ago, she said. A car accident. Not the accident itself. The lingering effects. You know how it is.

I told her I really admired her strength, and I actually meant it. Everyone in my life chose to run from the slightest hardship, either by sinking within themselves, or to the bottom of a bottle, or just getting in a car and driving away. Sasha was one of the first people I have ever met who knows that everything will be okay and sometimes all it takes is a little hard work. And having little people growing inside her helped, too, because she sacrificed for them, and now they sacrifice for her. It almost made me wish I had a child.

Just as my ovaries were second-guessing their purpose, a school bus stopped outside and three kids came running in through the back door. They didn't even seem bothered by a strange women sitting at the round table in the small kitchen picking melted cheese off a plate wearing clothes nearly falling off her body. The youngest girl introduced herself and showed me a drawing she did in class that day and was looking for nothing but praise, so I told her it was the most beautiful thing in the world, and it felt really good telling her that and seeing how it made her face light up. Sometimes telling lies is the best thing we can do for another person, especially a child.

The kids sat at the table, two across from me and the little girl beside me. The two girls asked me my name and how many kids I have and where I work and how I knew their mommy and what my favourite TV show is and if I wanted to come outside to play after dinner. The boy just stared at me. I don't think he was as impressed with me as the two girls, at least not in the same way. Sasha told them to stop pestering me and to go outside but I said I didn't mind and I let the little girl lead me by the hand to the backyard that was also fenced in with a chain-link fence and backed to another yard of a house that looked exactly the same.

The older boy and girl threw a ball back and forth and then to me and I threw it to the little girl but they told me she can't play because she's too young and too stupid to know how. The little girl didn't say anything and looked at her Velcro shoes and kicked at the rocks on the uneven concrete sidewalk steps leading up to the back door. I told them not to be mean and the little girl can play if she wants. The boy, the oldest, told me I didn't know what I was talking about because I didn't know anything about his family and threw the ball really hard at me, but I caught it, even though I don't think he expected me to.

You're not as good as you think you are, the boy said. And then he told me to take off my shirt.

I'm not taking off my shirt, I said.

Take it off. It's my brother's shirt. You're not allowed to wear it, so take it off.

I'm just borrowing it, I said. Your mother said it was okay.

It's not my mother's shirt. It's my brother's. It's his favourite shirt and you can't wear it. So take it off and show me your tits.

I couldn't help but laugh at this kid's boldness, remembering for a moment that children can be equally as terrible as any adult. The two little girls started laughing too, either with me or at the bad word the youngest girl kept repeating. I don't think the boy appreciated my laughing, because he grabbed the collar of the shirt and started to pull until it ripped. Hearing this, he let go and I was able to pull the rest of the shirt to my chest to keep him from seeing something to fantasize about for the rest of his adolescent life. The two girls ran for the house, the littlest one screaming that she was going to tell mommy. The boy and I just stood staring at one another, me holding his brother's shirt to my chest, him adjusting his shorts like the men in the laundromat, but with tears in his eyes.

Sasha came out and told the boy to get in the house and go to his room. She could not stop apologizing to me for her son's behaviour. She said he has always loved her firstborn but they don't get to see each other as much as they used to since her son moved out last year. I think he always sort of blamed me for that but I just couldn't find a way to explain that that happens as kids get older. And I definitely didn't want to tell him that one day he would leave too because I don't want to put ideas in his head and push him out sooner.

She looked at the tear in the collar of the shirt and apologized again when she saw I was still trying to cover myself. I told her it was fine but I could tell the tear tore at something in her and it really was her eldest son's shirt. She said she likes to wear it around the house because it reminds her of him.

Maybe you can fix it, I said.

Maybe I should just let it go.

Sasha said she cried for days when her son moved out, but she knew she just had to let him go.

In some ways, it's harder to let someone go who's still alive, she said. It's easier when you know that person is going to die.

He never got along with her second husband and she never blamed either of them for it. It was just a clash of personalities and DNA, she said. But I knew it hurt him, too. He was also in love and love makes fools of us all. He met his girlfriend in high school and after they graduated, they got it in their minds that they were going to get jobs and move in together and live happily ever after. I guess I should be proud of him for at least trying to make a life for himself. But I just worry. Especially since he started his new job.

What does he do? I asked.

He's a clerk at a convenience store not far from here. He's been working the midnight shift for a few weeks now. It just sounds so dangerous but he always tells me, Mom, don't worry, I'm fine. If anyone sticks a knife in my chest I'm told to just hand over the cash. No one will kill me for forty dollars. As though that's supposed to make me feel any better.

I tried to smile to hide my memories and guilt but I couldn't and instead I just said that I should probably get out of these clothes and back into my dress and Sasha showed me to the bedroom and closed the door part way.

I took off what was left of the driver's torn shirt who picked me up on the side of the highway and brought me back to his apartment while his girlfriend was away at work. I ignored the memories of him being upside down in a car in a ditch and Sasha laughing about how silly it was and his father hiding whatever pain he was feeling in his body, the after effects that either led to complications, drug addiction, or driving head-on into oncoming traffic. I put on my dress while looking at Sasha's closet of mostly sweatshirts, sweatpants, and a few dresses tucked in at the end of the rack. Pride and sorrow. Sasha's bag was on the dresser. I found the keys to the two-door, orange car, and opened the window and started to climb through but stopped when I noticed the youngest girl peering at me through the crack in the door.

Are you leaving? She whispered. I waved at her to come inside but she wouldn't, so I stood near the door and asked her to pull up the zipper on my still warm yellow dress. She said she really liked my dress and asked me what the mark near the strap was from. I told her I was in a car accident and she said that sounded scary.

It was, I said.

Are those mommy's keys, she asked, pointing to my hand. I told her they were and I asked if she wanted to come with me so no one would ever call her stupid ever again, even though that was hardly something I could promise. She started to push open the door when Sasha called to her to leave their guest alone and give her some peace. Her little face disappeared from the crack in the door and I went out the window, got in the small, two-door orange car, saw I had left the bag sitting on the passenger seat, and drove away.

I
MEET
VICTORIA'S
FATHER

on the top floor of the hospital on the east side of the city, the floor where the cancer patients receive treatment and wait to die, or wait to live, or wait for something, anything other than what they must be feeling, and I didn't want to come here, but Victoria insisted, and she helped me out of bed into the wheelchair and pushed along the pole with the IV bag that was still pumping me full of painkillers even though last week my body was pumped free of them, and it's a marvel to see how the modern medical system works these days as they fill you full of medications and then scold you when you're near-dead for taking too many, because it really is just a racket, the largest, most extensive racket in the country, but I'm not one to complain, because being in the hospital has always been like an all-expense paid vacation to a resort where the drugs are brought right up to your room and you just have to wait for the needle to be stuck into your hand, lay back, and watch terrible daytime TV and then be discharged with your own bottles of the same stuff, and be trusted not to take them all at once, and to be fair, I've only ever done that twice, and I doubt I will do it again, unless of course I happen to come across another woman in a yellow sundress and I happen to have a half-full bottle of painkillers, then I might again, but let's just hope that doesn't happen, but I can't shake the feeling that I might be getting ripped off and whatever these cancer patients are on must be really special, because seeing them, it's like they are dead already, and that's what every junkie wants, to get as close to death without actually dying, because someone must have started a rumour on the street one day that death is the greatest high there ever was, even though no one could ever really know that, unless they died and came back to life, or their heart stopped and they remembered some euphoric feeling of near death, but my heart has stopped numerous times and I don't remember feeling a goddamn thing, let alone euphoria, but then again, I've been extremely high on methamphetamines and morphine and lost days at a time, so maybe I have experienced the greatest high of my life and have just not been able to remember or appreciate it, but I don't say these things, because I have a feeling the patients dying of cancer and high out of their minds wouldn't really see it the same way a half-recovering, suicidal, former and current junkie who crashes cars on purpose does, and when Victoria rolls me into her father's room, his skinny, emaciated body hidden underneath a blanket, his face sunken and grey, his hair thin and translucent, I almost, almost feel guilty for the thoughts that drift in and out of my head, but I don't say this either and I don't say anything because even I know there are some situations that don't call for any words, but I do say thank you to Victoria for leaving me as far away from the bed as she can as she walks up to the side, runs her hand over the top of her father's head, and says, I'm here Daddy, and he tries to turn his head, he tries to open his eyes, and he tries to move his lips to say something, but he can't, and she tells him not to, and of course he doesn't listen because what he is trying to say could be the last thing he ever says to her, even though Victoria doesn't seem to think so because she is completely calm, her voice is soft, her face so gentle, and all I can think about is how loud that little voice in her head is screaming for a drink right now, just the constant yelling and demanding and pleading for just one drop of scotch, or vodka, or rum, or a beer, or hell, even rubbing alcohol, just a little taste to make it shut up, but she just keeps going, sitting down next to the bed, her hand still on his head, telling her father that she's here, that everything will be okay, and to not worry because he's not alone, and then she turns to me and says her friend is here to meet him, and he doesn't even try to turn his head toward me, and I'm not going to lie, I'm thankful for that, because to be honest, I don't even want him to know I'm there, the guilt is almost too much for me, and I don't know why I'm having all these feelings I haven't felt in years or ever, but it's all Victoria's fault, for screaming at me in the middle of the highway that night, for coming to the hospital and putting her hand on my arm, for taking me home to her apartment and running through routines with me and seeing me as a real person, and for calling 911 after I took the rest of my painkillers, and then coming to the hospital again to see if I was still alive, and for bringing someone who has tried to die more times than I can even remember to see a man who wants nothing more than to keep on living, and I try to excuse myself and wheel out of the room, but I don't have the strength and Victoria tells me to stay where I am, and she turns back to her father and starts talking to him again, telling him all about me, or what she knows, or what she think she knows, about how I'm a troubled person who needs to see what fighting really looks like, and who the fuck does she think she is to try and use her father as some kind of lesson for someone that doesn't care or is still feeling numb, for the most part, and a person who would have walked down this hallway before and not even noticed anyone was dying, but more so decaying from the inside, their bodies slowly eating them alive, and then carry on about my business of stealing bedside medications or testing IV drips, ignoring the boney hands the needles were pulled out of as though they didn't even exist, but now I have to sit here and stare directly at it, and I think I'm safe when Victoria stands up and walks back over to me, but we don't leave, she just wheels me to the side of the bed, right next to her dying father, and tells me to talk to him, and I tell her I don't know what to say, and she tells me to say whatever comes to mind, but if she only knew what went through my mind she would never ask me to do something so horrible and cruel to another human being, let alone her father, so I just say hello, and that he's looking well, and that he has a very kind and sweet daughter, the sorts of things a real person would say, but he doesn't say anything, he doesn't even try to, in fact, he just starts to move his head around, his eyes half open, looking for his daughter, and I tell him she is still here, and I motion to her to come next to me, but she doesn't move, she only tells me to tell him why I'm in the hospital, but I say it's none of his business, and Victoria comes back and I think she is going to wheel me away, but she just pushes me closer, and whispers into my ear to tell him why I want to die, and then she pulls the IV out of my hand, ripping the tape from my skin and allowing a little drop of blood to run between my fingers from the hole pushing out the last little bit of painkillers that were just being pumped into me, and Victoria whispers again that she wouldn't want me to be numb for this, so I tell her dying father that I'm in the hospital because I was in a car accident, but that's not good enough, that's a lie, and Victoria tells me this, so I tell her dying father that I'm in the hospital because I took half a bottle of painkillers, but this isn't good enough either, and Victoria tells me to keep going, but I have nothing else to say, I've already told the truth, I told him everything that happened, but she doesn't think I have, and she tells me to be completely honest with him, to tell him everything, not because he needs to hear it, but because I need to say it, so I tell her dying father that I took half a bottle of prescription painkillers because I saw a photo of a woman in a yellow sundress standing in front of a tree with Victoria in Stanley Park in 1992 and I remember seeing that woman's face illuminated by headlights before my car crashed into it going the wrong way up an off-ramp, or maybe she was, I can't really remember, and I wanted to get clean again but I don't like anything going to waste, so I swallowed the pills, and if I ever want to see her again, I just need to find a car, and drive until I do, and then I will know, one way or another, and Victoria's father isn't moving his head, or his eyes, or even trying to speak, but he seems more alive than he had been since I was wheeled in here, and

Victoria leans down again over my shoulder and whispers in my ear that she always hated that goddamn yellow dress.

Victoria wheels me down to the cafeteria on the second floor and parks me by the window. I'm trying to get the needle back in my hand but she tells me I should probably wait for a nurse to do that for me and then asks me what colour jello I want to eat. Green, I say.

I stare out the window, thinking about yellow dresses and the woman who wears one, and why she always seems to appear in my memories of broken glass and crushed metal and the taste of blood. Every single one I think of she's there. The time I crashed a stolen four-door burgundy Lincoln Continental into a pickup truck on a dark street across from the shopping mall, I can see her sitting in the middle seat between two ugly motherfuckers, her eyes wide open and so high above me when the truck, on raised struts, hit the corner of the hood and then flipped over and she disappeared. Or the time I hit a Pinto with some beat up Volkswagen on the highway and I blacked out from the airbag smashing into my face, I remember waking up and seeing someone running across the four lanes of the highway, the yellow dress fluttering in the wind from the passing cars. And the first time, the first accident I had ever been in when I was just sixteen-years-old, completely clean and sober and not yet knowing the life that was waiting for me, driving a station wagon, when a two-tone green sedan hit me from the side, sending my head through the window, and shattering my elbow, I remember seeing her there in the passenger seat, her body slumped over onto mine, the strap of the yellow dress falling down and a cut that started near her collarbone running all the way up and across her neck, and her eyes wide open and staring at me, her pupils dilated in the dim light, and a smile on her face.

Victoria returns and places the green jello on the table in front of me and takes the needle from my hand and stabs it into the plush armrest on the chair and tells me to leave it alone. She is sipping coffee that smells too strong and fiddles with a piece of jello between her finger and thumb that she took from my bowl.

I'm sorry about that, she says. I know it was hard, but I think you needed to say those things out loud.

I disagree and I'm tempted to tell her never to tell me to do anything ever again. And better yet, why doesn't she just fuck off and go get plastered in a bar down the street and pretend we never met in that church basement. It was all just a big mistake anyway. But I don't say those things, because I get the feeling that no matter what I say, it won't make a difference, she will never go away, like a voice in my head screaming for more.

I've never been an honest person, I say. So maybe I was lying.

No you weren't, she says. You know it and I know it.

But why him?

My father?

Yes, why him? Why make me say those things to him?

Because he's the only one who would listen isn't he? And he's the only one who would care. And to be perfectly honest with you, I've run out of things to say.

To me it didn't look like he cared at all. He barely moved and I don't even think he knew I was there, or Victoria for that matter. But she assures me that he did. He's not just an empty body waiting to fail, she says. He's still there, grasping at anything, even the smallest thing to know there's still a little life left out there.

And what did he grasp from me? I ask.

That you're a piece of shit, she says. And that he's lying there dying while you're still here. And that you will still be here for a long time. And that will piss him off and make him fight even harder so he can get better enough to sit up, stare you in the face, and tell you that you deserve to be where he is, not him. Or maybe it will just make him give up all together and question what life really means when there are others so willing to just throw it all away.

Is that what you want? I ask. For him to just give up so you can drink again?

It doesn't matter what I want.

Doesn't it to him? Maybe if you told him the truth he would just get it over with and die. For your sake.

He already knows the truth. And he knows yours as well. You haven't told him anything he hasn't heard before. But I think it's the first time you've heard it. Something even remotely resembling the truth.

Is that what you think? I ask.

It doesn't matter what I think. Is that you think?

No, I say. But I can tell Victoria doesn't believe me. I had twinges of guilt earlier when she first brought me there, and now I think she wants me to spill my guts, repent, tell her that I'm sorry for being the lowliest piece of human garbage that ever congealed out of the landfill, and then clean up my act, live a sober life of group meetings in church basements, and get a job, start a family, commute to work, and the only car accidents in my life will be the ones I pass on the highway and stare at like all the other people do, who either count their luck for not being the one still in the twisted wreck, or wish it was them.

But I won't do that, because I don't believe it. And I'm not sure what she wants me to say. I don't want to be like her father, or like any other poor son of a bitch lying in a hospital bed dying of cancer or any other disease, I want to die by choice, not by losing some unwinnable fight with some unseeable enemy. I want to die by turning a steering wheel or tipping a bottle back, but none of those things seem to work.

I know what you're trying to do, I tell her.

Oh yeah, what's that?

You're trying to make me a better person. You're trying to get me to see the light, or turn my life around, or to stop feeling sorry for myself. But what you don't understand, is there's nothing to turn around to. There is no light to see. And the last thing I feel is sorry for myself. So maybe you should focus on your own life, your own voice in your head tempting you to fuck up again, and I'll keep ignoring mine.

I would have wheeled away if I could, but I can't. Victoria only smiles, now eating the rest of my jello from the bowl with the plastic spoon.

Why aren't you asking me about her? she says, after squeezing the life out of the last green cube with her tongue.

About who?

The woman in the yellow dress.

I'm not asking Victoria about her because she only exists in my memory of cars and highways and off-ramps, not standing in front of massive trees in parks I will never see. I don't ask about her because if I do she will become real and at first I wanted to know if she was real or not, it's all I wanted to know, the only thing I could think about knowing, but now I want to keep the question alive. I want it to be like the voice in Victoria's head telling her to have a drink. I want the woman in the yellow sundress to keep showing up in car wrecks, real or imagined, and then to disappear, because it's the only thing that will keep me going.

I can tell you about her if you'd like, Victoria says.

I don't want to know.

I think you do.

I told you I don't.

Her name is Lola.

Her name is Lola. I think I already knew that.

I MEET VICTORIA'S FATHER ON THE TOP FLOOR OF THE HOSPITAL WHERE CANCER PATIENTS GO TO DIE,

the same place he has been in and out of four times in the last year, always getting better and then always getting worse, each time he comes back a little more of him is lost, until there will be nothing left, and I go with Victoria once a day to visit him the entire time I am in the hospital and every time I sit near the back and then I'm wheeled in closer so I can talk to him, face to what's left of his face, and every time I say a little more, every time I tell him about all the ways I've been broken, about the times I was found half-alive in a back alley with a needle in my arm, or about how I was found beaten and robbed in the bathroom of a convenience store, or how I stole a handgun from a pawnshop once and jerked a guy off for a bullet, and played Russian roulette for hours with a stray cat until its brains were splattered all over the brick wall of a restaurant on the city's south side, while my brains remained perfectly intact in my head leaning against the wall of a clinic, and I don't know if Victoria is listening to everything I'm saying, sometimes she's not even in the room, and one time when she isn't there, I lean in close to her father and tell him about Lola, and his eyes open and he looks right at me, turning his head to get a better look, the skin on his cheeks crinkling like paper, and I can see he is trying to say her name, and I tell him about how she's been with me during everything I have ever been through in my sorry excuse for a life, even if I think hard enough, I can see her walking away down the back alley while I push down the plunger on the needle, or see her peek in through the crack in the bathroom door in the convenience store to ask me if I taste the blood pouring from my nose, and I think that might have been her cat she lost, because I saw her calling its name down the street as I walked away feeling like there is nothing on this earth that can hurt me, or kill me, or destroy me, that I will keep on living long after everyone else is dead, and I tell this to Victoria's father, that I'm invincible, that I will never die and that Lola will always be there with me to keep me safe, and I love her for that, and I know she's real because she's there, in every single one of my memories, and I know she will be there again, I just have to get into a car and start driving, and keep driving until there's a gap in the oncoming lane and I can time it right to go up an off-ramp and I'll see her there again, in the driver's seat of an oncoming car, and we will meet in an explosion of electricity and light and then come back down to earth in the dark and sit next to one another, leaning against the railing of the off-ramp waiting for the flashing lights of emergency vehicles to show up and cut through the night, and we will both walk away and hold hands and kiss the blood from one another's lips, and then part ways and then do it all over again for the rest of time, and I want to keep going, I want to keep telling this dying man how everything in my life will be okay, but he's not looking at me anymore, his head is looking at the door and he's trying to speak and there is a tear coming from the corner of his grey eye, and he even tries to lift his arm, as though reaching, and I turn expecting to see Victoria standing there in the doorway, but all I see is a woman in a yellow dress.

I think her name is Lola.

I
MET
YOU

on the sixth floor of the hospital where my father went to die. You were sitting there in a wheelchair next to his bed. I couldn't tell who looked worse, you broken and wishing to fall to pieces or my father fighting to stay whole. I've been here before. I've waited in similar doorways, afraid to step inside. I've sat in the same wheelchair holding my mother's hand begging her to wake up. I've seen the same look of recognition in my father's eyes, followed by disappointment. I could tell he recognized me right away. He bought me this dress when I was sixteen and it was always my favourite because of how beautiful he said it made me look.

I'm not so sure you recognized me though. The way you looked at me, the way you stared, it was like you were trying to remember a dream that was mostly forgotten and the more you tried, the more distant it became. Our encounters were like a dream, distant memories we tried to place ourselves in again but just couldn't find the right space or the right feeling, so they were more like faded photographs with words on the back that we don't remember writing.

I had driven all night in Sasha's two-door orange car, up and down the highway, trying to decide whether I was coming into the city or still trying to leave it. I took off-ramps and on-ramps, mostly in the right direction, and I just kept driving because I didn't want to stop, I couldn't stop. The only thing that could stop me was you, crossing the centre line or going the wrong way up an off-ramp. Ever since we met that night on the off-ramp, I knew it was something more than a chance head-on collision on what is supposed to be a one-way thoroughfare. I had seen you so many times before. You were there beside me and you were there in front of me, your blank stare lit up by my headlights. You were in the back seat of a burning car my father and I passed on the highway when I was nine-years-old and he told me to look away. I saw you hanging upside down in a ditch with a mother, father, and young boy who was laughing at his mother's jokes but you never even smiled. You put a blanket around my shoulders to keep me warm on the side of the highway after I sideswiped a transport truck and spun around like a carnival ride. You were the only passenger on a bus when I ran a red light and smashed the teeth of a toothpaste model on the side. You were there in the only car across four lanes on the highway when I lost control and swerved right in front of you, the horror in your face matching my mother's scream perfectly.

And as much as I wanted to just keep driving, to keep replaying every single accident I've ever been in over and over and over again, I knew I would have to stop eventually. I couldn't just stay in this perpetual state of motion. I couldn't keep running forever, as much as I wanted to. I needed to find you because that is the only way I would ever stop searching. And there was only one way I knew how to find you.

All I could hope for was that the next set of headlights streaming through someone else's windshield would light up your face, so I just turned the wheel, closed my eyes, and hoped for the best.

But it wasn't you. It's never really you. It was some old woman driving back to town after visiting her grandchildren. I could hear her complain about her hip when the paramedics pried her door open. I was standing on the side of the highway a short distance away, leaning against the railing, waiting for the yellow flashing lights of a tow truck to pull up and take the broken two-door orange car away. When it finally came I walked back and got in the cab and the driver didn't say anything. He just finished securing the chains to make sure the twisted car wouldn't fall off the back and drove us away. No one even noticed I was there.

It's Trevor, right? I asked the driver. He made a little flourish with his hand over the white lettering stitched onto his blue overalls and then lit a cigarette filling the cab with a thin layer of smoke.

We've met before, haven't we? I asked. Trevor looked at me and smiled and then licked his top lip. It was then I tasted the blood still running from my nose over my mouth. I asked about you. I asked Trevor where you were and if you were okay. He opened the window, letting the passing air suck out all the smoke and whatever words he had to say, and then asked me if I was leaving the city or coming back to it, and if there was anything in the car aside from the bag on my lap.

How do you make a living off the broken lives of other people? I asked. He laughed and said he performs a necessary service.

You can't just leave wrecked cars on the roads, he said. The highway would be impassable in a matter of days. And besides, people don't like to see that. It reminds them of just how vulnerable they are out there driving. People like the illusion of safety.

And what about the things you steal? I asked him.

That's a rather nasty assumption, Trevor said. I'm a professional. Anything in the car is not my responsibility. Most things just get left behind on the highway. And besides, no one is going to miss anything. They have their lives, usually. That should be enough. And if they're dead, well then they definitely don't need anything anymore.

I asked Trevor if he remembered the night of our accident. He nodded his head and said he remembered. You were wearing the same dress, he said. I remember it really well.

Do you remember the second accident?

He said he remembered that one, too. It was a lot worse than the first. Then he said he's never known anyone to be in two different wrecks in the same day.

I was driving, I told him.

Well that explains it then.

Have you ever been in one? I asked.

A car accident?

Yeah.

No, I'm a safe driver.

Not everyone else is.

I know what to look for.

Headlights?

What's that?

You know to look out for headlights.

We pulled into the impound lot under the single flickering light and parked amongst rows and rows of crumpled cars and crushed SUVs and unrecognizable pickup trucks. Trevor turned off the truck and faced me.

What do you want? he asked.

I told him I wanted to know where you were.

I haven't the slightest clue, he said.

Aren't you worried?

Not even remotely.

Why? Everything that's happened to him is your fault. It's all your fault.

Is that what he told you? Did he tell you about all the car accidents he's been in, all the things he's stolen, all the drugs he's taken? It's interesting what some people choose to believe.

You mean me?

I mean him.

I looked away and focused on the inventory of memories in the yard hidden somewhere in all that metal and plastic and rubber. Memories of broken bones and broken lives. The last resting places of family photographs crushed on impact, letters spilled from gloveboxes blown down highways, irretrievable suitcases and purses trapped in trunks that no longer open, and small bags picked up and carried away never to be seen again.

You ought to be more careful, or you'll end up just like him, Trevor said.

Maybe that's not such a bad thing.

Oh it is. It very much is.

Why?
Because he's not a real person.

The last place I wanted to look was the one place I knew I had to. I've always hated hospitals, from the first time I was brought to one in an ambulance with a neck brace and a shattered femur that would require several pins and a metal bar and leave a long scar starting at the top of my knee to serve as a reminder of my mistakes, and my mother just ahead of me with severe head trauma from the impact. I would return to hospitals many times with minor cuts and bruises from fender benders or whiplash and concussions from being rear-ended or broken fingers and lacerations from rollovers and head-on collisions. But I stopped when my father was admitted to the hospital for the first time. It didn't take long to start again though. To get back behind the wheel because I couldn't handle seeing him there, going through that, dying for no other reason than living too long.

When he was admitted again Victoria told me things were going to be different this time. I asked her if she meant she was going to be sober. She slapped me across the face, said I was being selfish and that my addiction has taken years off his life, and that she never wanted to see me again. Our father was in the next room of the house we were raised in holding a small bag on his lap waiting for what would be his last trip. I knelt down in front of him and placed my hands overtop of his that were resting on the bag. I told him I was just going to put this in the trunk of the car with the rest of his things and I took the keys to Victoria's car and started driving.

I knew Victoria blamed me for our mother's death as much as I blamed myself. I was behind the wheel. She dealt with the loss by trying to find something to fill what was gone and that was alcohol. I dealt with the loss by trying to find something more. If you chase death long enough, it will find you eventually. It just takes one wrong turn. Not looking both ways. Drifting over the centre line. Driving the wrong way up an off-ramp.

So I just kept driving. I never knew where I was going. I never even knew where I wanted to go. I just knew I had to keep driving. As long as I was moving forward, I wouldn't have to worry about looking back, or caring about what the future held. My father was going to die. I knew that. And I knew I wouldn't be there. I didn't even say goodbye. My mother died but I had no way of knowing that. And I was there. But I didn't even say goodbye.

Every night I would be lost. How do you even get lost on the highway? I could never decide if I was leaving the city or returning to it. I just kept taking exits and driving for a little while, then taking another and another, going in circles down the highways, to the north, to the south, the east, and west. I kept going until one day I finally made a decision. I wasn't going to keep running. I couldn't. My mind was made up. I spotted a ramp on the other side of the highway and I crossed over four lanes of traffic. It was late. I didn't think I would meet anyone. But then I met you.

And then I met you again, there in my father's hospital room. Victoria was just outside in the hallway. She didn't take her eyes off me from the moment the elevator doors opened to when I walked up to her standing by the open door.

There's a stain on your dress, she said, pointing to the faded blood near the bottom. She always hated this dress.

I asked her how our father was and she said he's still hanging on, pointing to you sitting next to his bed.

I think he knows you, she said.

We've met before.

Victoria would tell me later that she brought you here after meeting you in a church basement trying to get clean or trying to take advantage of others who already had. I think he mistook me for someone else, she said.

Victoria had to go and claim our father's car from the impound lot. She searched for me, thinking maybe I was dead. But I wasn't in any hospital. I wasn't under arrest. I was just gone. She said the tow truck driver told her there was a woman in a yellow dress driving the car and that I left with you. She didn't know about the second accident until later, but she knew I was with someone, someone who was already broken, damaged, in pieces, which she knew would make me feel a little more whole because I've always been looking for that, for just one more accident so I could take the place of our mother. Broken people always show up at group counselling, she once said to me, and she begged me to come with her and before things fell apart she even wrote down the address of a church and the weekly schedule but I just left it in the car, refusing to admit that anything could help me because I never saw myself as broken on the inside, just on the outside. I wish you had come, Victoria told me. Maybe in a way you did.

I heard about what you did to her on the highway. I think she needed that. I think we all need that. I think that's what I've been chasing this entire time. I think we all need to feel a little helpless and not in control to really understand what being in control means. It means nothing. None of us are in control of anything.

You've known that all along, haven't you? That's why you live the life you do, if you can even call it living. It's more like surviving. You're a survivor, but the kind of survivor who walks out into the forest of his own free will and hopes to die, but always walks out on the other side. I've always hated that. Not that I keep walking in, but that I keep finding a way out. At least until we ran into one another. And now where are we? Stuck somewhere in the middle, unsure of which way to go to, how to pass through. I know you're in pain, or that you're numb, or that you have no control. Had I known you were out there, I might have been more careful.

But you were broken and I can only imagine you still are. After I saw you there in the room, next to my father, I wanted to walk up to you and tell you I was sorry for the things I said and the things I did and thank you for everything you had done for me. It was my fault. Everything was my fault.

But I couldn't. I couldn't face my father yet knowing he was dying. And I couldn't face you because then I would have to face myself and all the things I had done and still had to do until it was over. So I gave the bag to Victoria and told her it belongs to you and we found it in the trunk of a car. She knew I was lying but I could tell she didn't care. We both knew you needed it more than anyone else. So I watched her hand it to you and you pulling at the zipper but not hard enough to open it while staring at me standing in the doorway. Then you placed it on the side of the bed next to my father but I left before seeing if he reached for it.

I wanted to tell you everything that I had been unable to tell anyone else, even myself. But facing the truth, no matter how much we wish it wasn't real, is more difficult than pretending it's not.

I don't know what you remember or what you think you remember. But I hope the part you remember the most, what you will never forget, is that I'm real. That I was there. And if you need me to be there every time, I will be. I'll be wherever you need me to be. Because I know that you can't keep running. You can't trade your life for another. You can't take back what you've done or haven't done or wish you had done. You always just end up coming to a dead stop and then you have nowhere else to go. And severe head trauma, cancer, overdoses, car accidents, they can't save us, because life already has.

My father died last night. I just wanted you to know. He fought for a really long time and I think there was some relief that he doesn't have to fight anymore. Now we can go back to our lives. Our real lives, as real people, and decide if we are coming into the city or leaving, taking on-ramps and off-ramps, hypnotize ourselves in the taillights and be blinded by headlights, and just keep going forward until there's nowhere left to go.

I
MET
LOLA

on an off-ramp, on a highway south of the city, leaning against the railing, watching the emergency lights flash against the twisted metal of our two cars after coming into contact with one another in a head-on collision, either she was going the wrong way or I was, I can't remember, but it doesn't matter now, because she's here, with me, and she holds my hand, and I tell her I love her, and I taste the blood on her lips when we kiss, and she tells me that she needs to get as far away from here as she can and I never want to be away from her, so I will follow her everywhere she goes from now on, no matter what, whether it's leaving the city or coming into the city, whether she is hitching on the side of the highway or stealing two-door orange cars from mothers of three, or getting a ride with convenience store clerks working the midnight shift, all I know is I want to be everywhere she is, even if it's flying through the windshield of a smashed car, I want to see that yellow sundress on the other side, I want to see her everywhere I go, running across the highway and into traffic in the rain, I want to see her. I want to see her. I want to see her.

I MEET LOLA ON A ONE-WAY STREET ON THE CITY'S SOUTH SIDE, just across from a school where children can be heard playing through open windows during the day, and you can cross the street without looking because the traffic is so light and everyone drives slowly because it's a school zone and sometimes errant balls hop the fence, followed by children running after them, but in all the years the school has been there, not one child has been struck by a car, even though two cars collided there once, when all the children were outside, their games of hide-and-seek and red rover interrupted by the sound of two cars crunching together, and I can't remember if I crossed the centre line or if she did, but I remember seeing her there in the driver's seat, not looking ahead, looking to the side, at the children playing, and she was smiling, and her teeth cut into the airbag because she was still smiling when we hit, and when she got out of the car, she stood next to the fence, her fingers holding onto the metal, the children all running up to her because they could see the blood on the yellow of her dress, and I walked up to her and wrapped my arms around her from behind and told her that won't it be wonderful to have some of our own one day, and she touched her hand to my arm, and it's the greatest feeling in the world, and she smiles at me, and she tells me that she can't wait, and it feels like I'm already holding our child in her belly, and then she leans back, and kisses me, while all the children laugh and say that's gross, but I tell them I don't mind the taste of blood.

I MEET LOLA ON A SUBURBAN ROAD ON THE CITY'S WEST SIDE, the same neighbourhood where doctors and lawyers and accountants live, in gated communities, and pop-up mansions, with perfectly groomed lawns, and picket fences, and blue doors, and brick address monuments, the kind of place you would love to raise your children, the kind of place where teenagers feel suffocated, even though they secretly long to be like their parents, even if they say they want to live in the city, on the north side, or the south side, or any other side but the west side in these phoney affluent neighbourhoods where people pretend to be happy and flaunt their money because that's all they know to do with money anyway, and the streets are always quiet at all times of the day, but especially at night because no one ventures away from the safety of their homes past midnight, except of course for the drunk drivers returning home from office Christmas parties after drinking too many gin and tonics and hitting on co-workers, but once they get to the safety of the suburban neighbourhoods, they know everything will be fine and it's just a matter of navigating the many bends and cul-de-sacs and crescents until they find their home that looks just like everyone else's, and it's on one of these many twisting, bending roads that I met Lola, her driving a jet black BMW and me a classic Chevy Charger, and we are both driving too fast, and coming around one of the S curves in the road, and we are both too far over, and our faces are lit up before the driver side headlights kiss and we spin around and around and around, the street lights above us like strobes, and we come to rest facing the opposite direction we were travelling in, and there is a pause at first, a silence, and then Lola crawls out through the window, straightens her dress, music still coming from her radio because the key is still in the ignition and providing power to the car, and starts to spin around in the orange street lights above her head, and I crawl out through my window, and I wrap my arm around her waist and I take her hand, and we dance around in the empty street, the music playing in time to the dripping of gasoline and transmission fluid from the two cars still smoking, and if we listen closely, it almost sounds like applause from friends and family members, and I lean in and kiss her and feel the warmth of her blood against my lips and I tell her this is the happiest night of my life.

I MEET LOLA ON THE HIGHWAY LEADING INTO THE CITY, just far enough out that you can see the city lights turn the low lying clouds orange, and you know you will be home soon, because you can see the towers and the skyscrapers and the sprawling suburban neighbourhoods stretching out in all directions, and you even try to find the outside light of your house amongst all the others, but you can never really tell, so you just keep driving, knowing you'll be there soon, that it won't be much longer, and as you drive, you wonder where all the other cars leaving the city are going, why they're leaving, because it feels so good to be home, you don't know why anyone would want to leave in the first place, even though that was you just a week ago, headed away from all the hustle and bustle of city life, off to visit distant relatives or get away at the lake for a few days or just go on a road trip to see the lights of other cities appear on the horizon, even though they never feel quite as welcoming or like home like your city does, and I was driving, staring at the city lights, or was I staring at darkness, was I coming or was I going, I really can't remember, but what I do remember is seeing the sudden flash of Lola's face when she crossed the centre line and crashed head-on into my car, and as we both flew through the windshields, the seatbelts that gave way leaving long, jagged cuts from our collarbones across our necks, we look at one another, and blow each other kisses, and then we land on the pavement, metres away from the two cars that are now one, and we've never felt quite so far apart before, and neither of us can move to get closer, but we can still see one another, I can see her, lying there on the highway, the yellow dress fluttering in the wind from passing cars, and I whisper that I'm sorry, that I don't even remember what it was we were fighting about and I wasn't walking out on her and I can see her whisper back that she knows, she knows that I love her, and I would never do anything to hurt her, and even though we are on opposite sides of the highway and can't move, the blood coming from our necks and broken bodies spreading out across the pavement, we know we will always be together, and it's just a matter of time before the paramedics arrive, and lift us up, and maybe we will pass by each other again on the way to our ambulances, and maybe we will even get to reach our hands out, and maybe she will touch my arm, and then I will know everything will be okay.

I MEET LOLA ON A BUSY DOWNTOWN STREET IN THE CENTRE OF THE CITY,

in the financial district where skyscrapers block out the sun and the roads are always busy, no matter the time of day, and the sidewalks are full of people in fine suits and high-heeled shoes, and people in sleeping bags on sewer grates looking for a little extra change, and students walking to class, and tourists looking for the best place to eat, and every manner of real people going about their daily lives, waiting for the traffic lights, while cars honk and inch up and ride the bumper of the car in front of them, and it's actually one of the most likely places for car accidents just given the volume of traffic, but they are never very dramatic, but Lola and I never shy away from a show, so while I'm driving through an intersection, Lola, either not looking or not caring, turns in front of me and we collide, the front of my car striking the side of hers, and I push her all the way up onto the sidewalk, the tires screeching because they are no longer gripping the pavement, just sliding across it, and the car hops up and knocks over a lamp post and a mailbox and she is looking at me the whole time through the passenger-side window, and we come to a stop, she smiles, and she climbs out through the sunroof of the car, walks onto the hood of mine, and leans her head through the driver's side window from the roof of the car, and tells me she thinks I'm cute and asks if I want to grab a coffee, and I'm not one to say no to such a beautiful face, so I climb out through the window and we walk down the sidewalk as the sirens from the emergency vehicles fight to find a path through, and she takes my hand, and asks me where I want to go, and I say I don't care, and that I really love her yellow dress.

I MEET LOLA,
I meet Lola everywhere I go, any time of day or night, any situation, she's there, in that yellow dress, stained with blood, and we

always end up walking away together, because that's just how things are meant to be, and I can feel everything, the touch of her hand against my arm, the smell of the perfume on her neck, the taste of blood on her lips, and we just keep moving forward together, like a car on the highway, totally and completely in love, like it was meant to be, and no matter what happens, we will always meet again, somewhere, in some way, and I'm thankful for that, and I want to feel everything, I want to be a real person, I want to know that all I have to do is look up and I will see her there and then I will know everything will be okay, because she's been with me every step of the way, and so now, while I drive down the highway at full speed, not looking for anything in particular, just driving to drive, maybe leave the city, maybe come back to it, it doesn't matter, for the first time I actually feel like everything is right, that there's nothing to run from, nothing to hide from, that everything really will be okay because she said it will be, and as I drive, smiling to myself, thinking about how wonderful it is to have someone so amazing, so beautiful in my life, I don't see a car cross over the centre line, and I don't feel the impact right away, I only hear the sound of crushing metal and broken glass, and the feeling of being spun around and around, until everything comes to a complete and sudden stop, and I wonder if this is where sobriety has taken me, and it almost seems ironic, but I was never one for irony, so I sit in the car, my head on the steering wheel above the deflated airbag, and wait for the emergency lights, and from where the cars ended up, from where my head is facing, I can't see who is in the other car, and I can't move, I can't even turn my head, so even though I'm sure she is there, I can't see her, I can't even call out to her, and when the red lights illuminate the inside of my car, I see her, or I think it's her, there is a flash of yellow through the broken windshield, and the door is pried open and I see a woman in a yellow raincoat, even though I don't think its raining, and she tells me that everything will be okay, and I try to read the name on the little patch above her breast, but it's too dark and I can't make it out, and I ask her if Lola is all right, but she tells me not to worry about anyone else, because they are going to take care of me, but I want to know if Lola is all right, and I can hear them prying open the other car, and then the unmistakable counting of someone trying to breathe life back into another body, and I can't stop laughing and the paramedic tells me to calm down, that everything will be all right, and I try to turn my head to see if anyone was sitting next to me, or I try to remember if I was sitting there and someone else was driving, but I can't remember if I was driving or not, or if I was going in the wrong direction or Lola was, and the paramedic in the yellow raincoat even though it's not raining, with a name I can't quite make out, tells me to remain calm, and I tell her to check the trunk of the car and she tells me not to worry about that, and that everything is going to be okay, everything is going to be just fine.

Check the trunk of the car. There's a bag in the trunk of the car.

ACKNOWLEDGEMENTS

I would like to thank all of the organizers, judges, and volunteers at the 3-Day Novel Contest, and Anvil Press. Congratulations to all the writers who participated in the 42nd Annual 3-Day Novel Contest. As always, you are all literary warriors and should be proud of what you have accomplished. Thank you to Brian, Jess, and Karen at Anvil Press for all their help, guidance, and making this possible. And once again, a big thank you to Derek von Essen for another great cover.

Thank you to all the members and board of the Northwestern Ontario Writer's Workshop for all your support and encouragement and for fostering the growth of writing in Northern Ontario. And thank you to all those who supported my first novel, *Chalk*, including the Ontario Library Service who selected it as the 2016 winner of the Northern Literature Award.

A special thank you to Alana Pickrell for convincing me to enter the contest again and encouraging me to keep going every step of the way. This wouldn't be possible without you. And finally, as always, thank you to my family for all their love and support, who continue to be proud of me no matter what I do, and for teaching me the value of reading, writing, and being myself.

Doug Diaczuk is a journalist and photographer living in Thunder Bay, Ontario. He has a master's degree in English Literature and his work has been published in *Quill and Quire*, *Geist*, and *subTerrain*. His first novel *Chalk* was the winner of the 38th Annual 3-Day Novel Writing Contest, and went on to win the Northern Lit Award in 2016.